Angels Have the Last Laugh

Angels Have the Last Laugh

The Chronicles of a Guardian Angel

Alberta Rothe Nielson

CFI
Springville, Utah

© 2006 Alberta Rothe Nielson

All rights reserved.

No part of this book may be reproduced in any form whatsoever, whether by graphic, visual, electronic, film, microfilm, tape recording, or any other means, without prior written permission of the author, except in the case of brief passages embodied in critical reviews and articles.

ISBN: 1-55517-923-1
e. 1

Published by CFI,
an imprint of Cedar Fort, Inc.
925 N. Main, Springville, Utah, 84663
www.cedarfort.com

Distributed by:

Typeset by Natalie Roach
Cover design by Nicole Williams
Cover design © 2006 by Lyle Mortimer

Printed in the United States of America
10 9 8 7 6 5 4 3 2 1
Printed on acid-free paper

Dedication

To my mother,
Jennie Catherine Adams Rothe.
The best.

The nature of things:
Facts do not cease to exist
Even when ignored.

Contents

Acknowledgments xi
Prologue xiii

Henry Is Gone 1
The Longing 17
The Little Green House. 23
Something Grabbed My Pen 41
The Last Chicken 48
Be Still and Listen. 50
Ode to the Pearl of Great Price 56
The Country Store. 60
My Book of Life .69
Befuddled 71
This Leaf. 77
The Crash 79
Epilogue 90

Acknowledgments

Many thanks to those who have helped me make my messages flow with the proper commas, dashes, and quotes in the right places—my son Ron Nielson and my neighbor Barbara Wand. Thanks also to those of my children who have reviewed and given me the okay to write our stories—Toi, Rico, Ray, Peggy, Guy, Victoria, and Ed. Most of all, I give thanks for life—life that brings opportunities and experiences for making good stories and memories and that allows me the courage to break the veil of dreams and dare to step out of my comfort zone into the marvelous world of enlightenment.

Prologue

I sometimes wondered if there were angels. Sometimes brilliant thoughts would pop into my mind, and I would wonder where they came from. My mother would say, "Your guardian angel told you that."

"Are there such things?" I asked her.

"I believe that there are angels around us."

"Have you seen them?"

"No, I have not seen them, but sometimes when I am very happy or very sad I feel a presence and wonder if they are really there. Just believing that they could be there gives me comfort and helps me to be a better person."

She was right; they are there. I know because now I am one.

Let me introduce myself. My name is Randolf Rippenhoffer. Please call me R^2 for short. That is pronounced R squared. You see, as a kid, they called me RR for short. And then when I became an engineer they used a math term called R x R or R^2. Say that several times so you get used to saying it, R squared, R squared, R^2, R^2, R^2.

While golfing with my grandson as a mortal, I had a heart attack right there on the golf course. He took me to the hospital where I noticed a bright hole in the corner of the room. I was so attracted to it that soon I realized I was right up there checking it out—actually floating around at the top of the room. I felt so light and airy. The ultrabright light in the hole was like a magnet, pulling me closer and closer. It drew me right to it and then, it drew me right through it. That is how I became an angel.

There I received an assignment to go back to earth to guide and assist mortals on their blinded path through mortal life. By blinded I mean that when mortals are born, a veil is placed over the memory of pre-earth life—that wonderful pre-earth-life memory of how great it was to live in the presence of God. Now, on their own, they must find their way back.

Angels can help if mortals listen to their promptings and still, small voices. Even a spark or two may be felt to get the person's attention. We can even muddle their minds when they are on the wrong path to let them know that is a wrong choice.

Angels are known by other names too. They could be known as a Higher Power, Luck, or Lady Luck, depending where one believes his inspiration comes from. I call it an angel because I am one.

I have already served one mission as a guardian angel. Some of those I helped would listen to me, and some would not. I laughed with some of them, and I cried with some of them. My report is in a book called *Angels Can Laugh Too*. I was able to go home for some R & R, and now I am on my second mission. Henry gave me such a hard time before, so now I am eager to try him again.

Perhaps I will meet *you* sometime when you shouldn't have had your hand in a cookie jar.

Listen up. —R^2

Admonishment
Danger signs that make you slip
Always be aware

Henry Is Gone

Henry was gone. At least I could not find him on his favorite stool at the end of the bar. I rushed to his home. Not there. Mary was gone too. Are they on vacation? Visiting a friend? Meeting with family? These questions continued to rotate in my mind. A note by the phone said Mary had called a taxi. The hospital. I dropped in (I can do that, you know, because I am an angel) and found him on the fourth floor in room 402. That couldn't be Henry lying there, I thought. It doesn't look like Henry lying there. It looks like a crookneck squash—yellow as all get-out. "Henry, Henry," I called out to him. "What is going on here?"

"My liver, I have ruined my liver."

"What happened?"

"R^2, you know what happened. I should have stopped drinking when you tried to get me to stop. I was going to; I really meant to. But I was like Saint Augustine of old, who asked the Lord to 'please make me perfect,' and then added, 'but not quite yet.' That is how I felt; I wanted to stop drinking—but not quite yet. 'Tomorrow would be a good day to stop,' I told myself, 'or maybe the day after tomorrow would be even better.' Now I am forced into that day, and it is too late."

"I'm so sorry, Henry."

"Just look how yellow I am, even my eyeballs. Can you believe that?"

"Why are your eyeballs yellow? What makes you yellow?"

"The doctor said that alcohol has injured my liver. It hardens the cells so they cannot work properly. The yellow bile ducts become blocked so the yellow filters through the body."

"Did you have any early symptoms to let you know what was happening?"

"There are no symptoms in the early stages until the liver function starts to fail. Then I started feeling tired and weak. I lost weight. I lost my appetite. I became nauseous."

"Henry, you should have gone to the doctor sooner when you first started feeling sick."

"I did."

"What did the doctor say?"

"He told me that my liver was like a tree with lots of beautiful green leaves. Then he added that each time I took a drink of alcohol I lost one leaf."

"That is a good way to explain it. How is your tree now?"

"It is bare. The leaves are gone."

"I was afraid of that, Henry." I sat in silence and just didn't know what to say to him. He looked so hopeless, and I could feel his utter depth of discouragement. Questions flowed through my mind. Why does this have to happen to such great people? How does one fall into such a trap? When is one in too deep? Where does one turn for help? What can I say to him? Such questions must have answers.

"You have always been a good kind of fellow, Henry, so why does this have to happen to such great good people?"

"TV ads make parties look so fun; the boys are good looking and the gals are skinny."

"Did you chum with good-looking guys and skinny gals?"

"No. Just old guys like me who told stories of how just a couple of drinks relaxed them so they were not so shy."

"Were you shy, Henry?"

"Yes, I was kind of shy, but I found just a couple of drinks could relax me so I could be one of the group."

"Was it fun being part of the group?"

"There is a special feeling of being part of a group like that. It was a kind of social club."

"If it was a social club, wouldn't you want to include your wife? Why didn't Mary go?"

"I tried to get her to go, but she never wanted to."

"Did she give you a reason why?"

"When she was a girl, her mother told her how drinking makes you lose control of yourself, and she did not want to let that happen. She did go with me one time and felt very uncomfortable when everyone else was drinking. I told her that a couple of drinks would loosen her up.

"She was very adamant when she said, 'Henry, I do not want to drink!' She told me that she felt very awkward—felt like a dud."

"A dud?"

"R^2, she told me that it was not good to mix drinkers with nondrinkers."

"Why?"

"She said that it was like having tall basketball players compete against short basketball players. The tall ones take over, and the short ones feel like duds because they can never get their hands on the ball. They are not really duds; they just feel like duds in that kind of a situation."

"Yes, I can picture that."

"Mary said that it is the same with drinkers and nondrinkers; with nondrinkers around, the drinkers feel somewhat conscious about drinking even though they are having such a lack-of-control time. It is awkward. Then after a few more drinks, they have forgotten about the nondrinkers, who, by this time, feel like duds."

"Henry, before you started drinking did you feel like a dud?"

"Yes, I felt awkward."

"At that time, you should have drawn away instead of joining them." Henry was silent. I continued, "Were they good people?"

"Of course they were good people."

"So, what is the answer, Henry? Why do bad things happen to good people?"

"There are good people on both sides. But to be comfortable, one must make a choice between the two. Nondrinkers can have a great time too, and in the morning they still remember what fun they had."

"Yes, I have heard that comment before, in jest of course, but there may be some truth in it."

Henry was quiet for some time. I could see that he was deep in thought. Then he added another thought.

"Mary reminded me often that my habit cost too much money."

"Does it cost a lot of money, Henry?"

"Oh yes. It is a terrible waste of both time and money."

"Then why did you continue to drink?"

"That is what I ask myself all the time." There was another deep-thinking pause.

I asked, "Henry, when I saw you at the club, I didn't see your group. Where were they?"

"After a little time, I found that the group was not so much fun after all. All I wanted was my beer, so I sat alone."

"You thought you were sitting alone at the bar, Henry, but there was someone with you. I saw them."

"You saw them? Who were they?"

"They were like me."

"Well I don't ever see you, R^2. I only hear your words."

"They gave words to you too."

"What did they say?"

"Don't you remember hearing the thoughts such as 'Just one more drink, Henry, and then you can go home,' or 'Your wife is probably asleep by now, so you don't have to hurry home,' or 'Henry, you have worked hard all day, and you deserve to stop in at the bar,' or 'Only a couple and then you can go home,' or . ."

"Yes, those were my thoughts."

"No Henry, they were not your thoughts. Those thoughts were their thoughts—negative, to keep you at the bar." Henry sat silently, and I could see that he was deep in thought. I continued, "Do you know, Henry, that the first time I saw you they were with you? Three of them. They are like me, except they try to get people to sin and do harmful things. They can put words in your thoughts just like I can. They want you to stay because they feel like they are drinking through you. I could see that their lips were trying to get to your drink. Of course, they couldn't, but they were trying."

I paused to see how he was taking it. He seemed to be understanding all right. Then I added, "You may be relieved to hear what I have to say. Henry . . . when they saw me, they backed away. Do you know that they were afraid of me?"

"Afraid of you?"

"Yes, that should tell you that positive thoughts are stronger and better than negative thoughts. Both can be there, so when you hear them you must make a choice."

Then I changed the subject. "Henry, when did you know you were in too deep?"

"I knew that I was in too deep when I felt I was trapped and couldn't get out."

"You can get out, Henry, but it is not easy. I will help you."

"No, I am afraid that this is it."

"This is what?"

"You know what I mean." Then he asked, "Are you here to escort me home to that place where you are from? Wherever it is?"

"No, Henry, I am not here to take you away, I am here to help you get better."

"You are a dreamer."

"No, not a dreamer, I am a positive nudge in your conscience. If you will just let me stay, I can help you."

"You are always welcome to stay, but I know now that I am a goner."

With that negative thought Henry tuned me out, so I turned to Mary. Dear Mary. She had been through so much. It was not easy living with someone like Henry. It wasn't Henry, per se, as Henry was a good man; it is what Henry had allowed to happen in his life. Mary had become second fiddle to the bottle. At times she felt like she was walking on eggs so as not to offend him. His pleasant mood could change to a harsh one at the flip of a switch. It had been difficult living with him. Now here she was, faithfully sitting at his bedside, waiting, wondering, and hopelessly fearing what might come next.

"Mary," I said, "Can you hear me?" Mary shifted in her chair, so I continued. "You are like an angel sitting here with your dear Henry. Many times you waited for him to come home, and when he did, you faithfully took off his shoes and put him in bed. That has not been easy for you, Mary. You are a gem. Perhaps I can help, Mary. I have an idea. Find an interesting book and start reading to Henry."

"He is always sleeping."

"He looks like he is sleeping, but sometimes he is just closing his eyes and thinking of what he wishes he had done differently. Those sad thoughts can be pushed away with thoughts from a good story."

I could see new life come into Mary, and she said, "I can do that." She sat by Henry's bed and put her hand on his arm. He stirred, so she knew he was awake. Mary continued, "Henry, can you hear me?" She saw a positive nod of his head. "Henry, would you like to hear a story?"

"I need to sleep."

"Yes, you do. Just sleep all you want to, but when you are awake, I would like to share stories with you as we used to do long ago. Remember the fun we had taking turns reading to each other? I have a book here that sounds so interesting."

So the book reading began. I was pleased with that. I could see that Henry was listening, and I could sense that he was enjoying it. At times the story was pushing out the helpless thoughts, yet at times the helpless thoughts took over again. After a few pages, Mary noticed that his breathing got heavy and then heavier, so she knew he was really asleep. She put the book down and waited. She was used to the waiting part. Over the years she had waited and waited and wondered when Henry would ever come home. He always did. She had always been thankful that at least he came home. She hoped that he came home to her and not just to a bed to sleep.

There was some reading and sleeping, taking turns as the days went by. She read, and he listened when he was not sleeping. Though Mary kept reading to him, there had not been much effort on Henry's part to show any enjoyment. She even wondered if the reading was really worthwhile. But I encouraged her to keep reading because I could see that Henry was listening and improving. This became apparent to Mary, when one day to her surprise as she walked into the room Henry was reading the book himself. Her heart leaped with joy. Henry's attitude had changed. He looked like he now had a desire to live. He was starting to heal.

A week later, Mary talked to the doctor at the nurses' station. The doctor looked somber but was trying to be positive by giving some good news. "Henry can go home now," he said. "You can take him home, Mary. I will release him tomorrow."

Mary was puzzled. She knew that Henry was doing a lot better but not enough to go home. The many pills he was taking seemed to be helping him. Much of the yellow color was fading. With a puzzled look, she asked, "Is he actually well enough to go home? Will he be okay?"

The doctor was quiet.

Mary continued, "He doesn't look quite well enough to me."

The doctor advised, "Just have him take the pills I have given you. They seem to be helping. Then we can go from there."

"Go from there!" Mary said, "What does that mean?" She was aghast. I was aghast. We were both struck dumb with the horror of his statement. What *does* that mean?

With further thought, I caught the drift of the doctor's comment and broke into Mary's thought. "Mary . . . maybe there is nothing more he can do for Henry. Mary . . . maybe he is sending Henry home to die."

Mary caught her breath. Anger showed in her voice as she looked straight into his eyes and asked point-blank, "Are you sending him home to die?"

I had planted that thought into her mind but did not realize that she would be so bold as to ask it. They were harsh words.

My heart went out to the doctor as I watched him bow his head. He was a good doctor, a kind doctor, one who has mastered the right words to ease a bad situation. But these harsh words surprised him. "That is a hard question to answer," I whispered to him. He gently echoed it.

But Mary was worried. She was afraid. She wanted an answer, so she cried out, "You think that is a hard question to answer; it is an even harder question to ask." Mary's hands covered her sobbing. When she lowered her hands from her face, she pleaded, "I must know."

There was a long, awkward pause. Time stood still as if a void dominated the whole hospital. Finally, the doctor broke the silence. His eyes were full of compassion; his voice was tender. "Mary . . . I have done all I can do. We just have to wait and see how he responds to the medication I have prescribed."

Mary gained control of her emotions again and realized that now she would be Henry's caretaker at home. "What should he eat?" she asked.

"He can eat anything he wants, anytime he wants."

"Can he get up now? Should he walk? Will he—"

"Mary," interrupted the doctor, "He can do anything he wants—walk, sit, run, jog, laugh. Keep him positive and happy. Make sure that he takes all the pills as directed."

"Will he really get better?"

"The pills have made a difference already. His yellowness is fading. We just have to wait and see how he responds."

So Henry came home. This time his bottle was filled with pills.

Days followed days, and sweet Mary was always at his side. I tried to help Henry where I could. Once I asked him to think about his childhood. The first thing that came to his mind was the school he went to.

"What kind of school was it?" I asked.

"A country school—only two rooms and eleven grades."

That was a surprise to me. "How can eleven grades fit into two rooms?"

"Six grades in one room and five in the next room."

"What happened to the twelfth grade?"

"If you got that far, you had to go to a bigger town."

"How many teachers did you have?"

"Only two teachers, one in the little room and one in the big room."

"Was one room smaller than the other?"

"No, they were the same size. The little room was for the little kids and the big room was for the big kids."

"That makes sense," I said. "But how can one teacher teach six grades?"

"Very carefully," he answered while smiling. "I mean, it took lots of organization. For instance, each grade had one row of desks—about five desks in each row. The first grade was the first row, the second grade was the second row, and so on. Each year when I graduated from one grade, I simply moved one row back. All the grades moved back and then the sixth graders went to the first row in the big room and the new first graders got the first row in the little room."

"Sounds pretty confusing to me; how could you learn with all that noise going on?"

"I got used to it. Say that I was in the fourth grade. When I got to school, I would go to my desk. On the blackboard at the front of the room was an assignment for me to start working on. Each row had its own assignment. Right away we were all working quietly while the teacher started teaching the first grade. It worked very smoothly. Watching the teacher teach the first grade was more interesting than my work, and it was difficult to not watch. If the teacher saw me watching, she would give me that *teacher look*. If I did not respond immediately, I usually got a piece of chalk or whatever was handy thrown at me. Especially I remember Miss Cox—her aim was right on. We all learned to duck those missiles because watching the little kids learn their letters and numbers was so interesting."

His eyes smiled when he added, "Then one day Miss Cox had a young boy who had a hard time with remembering words in his reading. He would sound out a couple of letters and say that much, but by the time he sounded out the rest of the word he had forgotten the first part. This time the teacher took him up to the blackboard and wrote the word 'help' for him to read. Again, he had that same problem. Finally she covered the 'p' with her hand and asked him to sound out the 'hel' part. He finally got that down good. I was feeling so sorry for him; he showed such frustration. I had a hard time not watching. Several times he read the uncovered 'hel' part. Then the teacher took her hand off the remaining letter and told him to add the 'p.' But the boy, thinking that 'hel' was a swear word and that was what the teacher was trying to tell him, just said another swear word. We all giggled. We couldn't help it." Henry actually laughed out loud. Mary heard and was pleased.

"That must have been some teacher," I said.

"Especially Miss Cox," he continued. "She was short—not much taller than the biggest little kids in our room. But oh, was she feisty. During our recesses, she would come out on the playground and join in our games, but the minute she rang that big old cowbell to call us back to class, we all knew who was boss. She was my favorite teacher of all. Now as I look back to those small classes, I think they were better than today."

"Better than the bigger classes of today?"

"Yes. Say I was in the fourth grade and sitting right in the middle of the third and fifth grades. If I forgot something I learned in the third grade, I could catch it again by listening to the teacher teach them. By the same token, some of the teaching in the fifth grade would rub off on me, and I would know what was coming next year."

"So in this way, you were really learning something three times."

"Right. And in the meantime, I learned to do my work or studies amidst a lot of noise and commotion. I learned to weed it all out."

"So your concentration was developed through that little two-room-school experience. What great memories you—"

Henry's thought process interrupted my words. "The peanut bust was my favorite school activity."

"Peanut bust?"

"You mean you never ever had a peanut bust in school? I thought all schools had peanut busts."

"Nope. Tell me about them."

"We had a little country store where we could buy peanuts. One of the big kids would tell us to buy a bag of peanuts and hide them in our desks at school. On a signal from that big sixth grader, we would all throw peanuts at the teacher."

"Didn't that hurt the teacher?"

"I think that they must have stung some because the teacher would turn her back to us until the blast was over. She reminded me of the cattle in a winter storm—they always turned their back-ends to the wind to protect their heads. I guess the teacher did the same to protect her head. Then when the peanut blast stopped, we would drop to the floor and gather as many peanuts as we could and then talk and laugh while eating them. It was great fun. Of course shells were all over the floor, inches thick. You can bet that the rest of the studies were over for that day. It was even fun sweeping up the mess and throwing the peanut shells in the pot-bellied stove in the corner of the room. The flames would flare up like it was eating candy."

"You paint a good picture, Henry. I can just see those little kids peppering the teacher with those peanuts. But did she ever get mad? You know—make you stay after school or no recess or something?"

"R^2, remember that these were the good, old-fashioned teachers, good sports, always ready for a fun time with the children. As a student, one always knew when it was time to study and when it was time to play. With children of multiple ages and grades, there had to be strict rules in the classroom. My teachers would play games with us at recess and be as rowdy as the children, but the minute the big old hand bell rang for class, everyone knew who was the boss. So teachers expected and loved peanut busts too because they were a tradition in my old country school.

"I like that, Henry. Could that happen today? Perhaps if the teachers would play more with their students. I would call it a relationship—teachers need to develop a relationship with each student. Students may respond better to the difference between study time and play time. As an angel, I can see the need for more relationship building.

"I had a teacher who was a good sport. I was in eighth grade. My room was full of eighth graders—about thirty of them—not just five in a row as you had. It was the last class at the end of the day, and I was getting tired of listening. I jumped up out of my desk and shouted, 'Everyone hold still; I lost my contact lens. It must be on the floor somewhere.' Students carefully dropped to the floor in search of it. After about twenty minutes, the buzzer rang, and school was out. I think the teacher suspected something, but she let it go with a laugh and a hope-you-find-it-soon look.

"Later that month, my mother was at the parent-teacher meeting, and my teacher asked my mother if I had ever found my contact lens. My mother was surprised and said, 'He doesn't wear contact lenses.' Oh, was I ever in trouble."

Henry laughed again, a big one this time, and said. "You did that, and now you are an angel?"

"Just one of my foibles as a teenager. I guess I was forgiven. It takes time for teenagers to grow and find a place in life where they feel comfortable. There are so many good and bad choices made at that time. Hopefully it all comes out in the wash, and they end up okay."

I could see that Henry was getting tired and needed

to sleep. He looked so peaceful lying there with his memories. Good memories comfort us. I turned to his wife.

"Mary, I am glad that you are here with Henry. I find that he always looks better when he is thinking about the fun old days, so try to keep him telling you stories. Make sure that he takes his pills. I will be back sometime later. The 'sometime' is something that I cannot decipher because I work in a different time frame than you do. But I will be back."

I dropped in again one day, and as before, there was no one home. I quickly headed for the bar. He wasn't there either. I hurried back to their home and by the phone was a note saying, "Barbados, here we come." A smile touched my whole face. Angels can smile, and I smiled.

I dropped into Barbados and there they were, exiting a cruise ship, walking down the gangplank arm in arm. People of shiny, dark skin were greeting them with treasures of that beautiful land for sale.

"Henry," I called, "Who is that beautiful woman on your arm?"

He stopped. Mary gave him a puzzled look. Henry looked into her eyes and said, "I just thought of how lucky I am to have such a beautiful woman on my arm."

"Oh, Henry, stop that. You make me feel silly."

"Well, you are beautiful," he said as he put his arm around her.

"But here—right in the middle of all these people."

Henry looked serious. "Mary, as I walked down that gangplank, I thought of why we are here."

"Now, Henry, you don't have to mention that again."

"But how did you ever have the courage to stay with me and then to save all that money?"

"R^2 is to blame."

Henry was surprised. "R^2? You know R^2?"

"Of course I know R^2. That is why I have stayed beside you all this time. He even suggested that I set aside the same amount of money that you spent, just in case."

Henry drew her closer to him and held her tight. The shiny, dark faces grinned, and so did I.

I would like to report that due to the selflessness of his dear wife, Mary, and his faithful attendance at community programs, Henry is still dry.

"Hang tight, Henry," I admonished, "and recognize the danger signs that cause you to slip."

I planted these words in Henry's memory to help alert him to the danger. —R^2

A natural growth
Not made. Developed through time
A Woman, it is

The Longing

At age eight, a little girl sat on the curb in front of the temple. She had dark brown curly hair with ringlets at the back. Her hair was oh so curly that the ringlets would not hang down—they would pull up and curl snugly around her neck.

I knew who she was and why she was sitting there. Her friends were in the temple being baptized—eight-year-old-boys and girls. She was not one of them; she was left out. It was the custom, at that time, for eight-year-old children to be baptized in the temple. It was also the custom for the whole Primary class to wait until all the children turned eight years old; then all would go to the temple together.

The children were from Kimball, a small town in southern Alberta, Canada, a farming and ranching community. In fact, if you blinked while driving by, you might miss it. Most of the children rode horses to school (but that is another story). The town had just one store, which included the post office, gas pump, and the aromas of everything from dill pickles in a crock to coal oil for the lamps. Even the dentist dropped in with his foot-pedaled drilling machine. It was the gathering place for farmers and cowboys to catch up on the local news.

The temple was in another town, Cardston, which had blocks of stores and several gas pumps, even a theater with an ice cream and candy store next door. It was ten miles from Kimball.

There Sally sat, waiting for her friends to come back out of the temple.

"Do you wish you were with them?" I asked. She could not see me, but I could speak to her in her mind. I can do that, you know, because I am an angel. "My name is R^2," I said, introducing myself to her. Again I asked her, "Sally, do you wish you were with them?"

She nodded her head up and down. "Then why aren't you with them?" I quizzed.

"Their church is not my church."

"Were you ever invited to go to their church?"

"Yes, sometimes in the springtime. It was lots of fun."

"Why the springtime?"

"Because most of my friends went to church on Sunday and then on Wednesday afternoon our school class would be let out early so we could go to what they called Primary. We would run out the school door, across the grassy field, even stop to pick a buttercup or two, and on to the church."

Thoughts continued going through Sally's mind.

"Dad said that I could go with the children on Wednesday; otherwise, I would just have to sit and wait for my older brothers to get out of school so we could ride the horse back home."

She remembered, "One time I asked Dad if I could be baptized."

"What did he say?"

"He said that my friends' church was not his church." Then she continued, "He said that the people in the church were good people, and it would be good for me to go with my school friends on Wednesday."

"Does he go to his own church?"

"No. But he did as a kid. He said that he was confirmed as a teenager and that was—enough—church—for—him." I laughed. That sounded like a teenager.

A girl, about Sally's age, who lived across the street from the temple, saw Sally sitting there. Soon there were two little girls sitting on the curb in front of the temple. Sally shared her story about why she was sitting there. The new friend said that she had already been baptized. She told Sally how she loved living across from the temple. She could even see it from her bedroom window. At night she especially loved it because the lights of the temple shone way up high in the sky. It even lit up her room. She loved sleeping in the light of the temple. It made her feel safe.

She explained how pretty it was inside the temple. She had only been in there that once, but she remembered that the beauty of it took her breath away. She shared her experience of being baptized. She was dressed all in white. So were the other people. The baptismal font was like a round bowl resting on the backs of twelve big oxen. Only their heads and front legs could be seen. The water was so warm. A man held her hands tight, said a prayer, and dipped her back into the water. Every part of her had to be under the water. One of her friends let one toe stick up out of the water, so they had to dip her again. Sally listened. She wished so much that she could be part of all that too.

I had an idea. I left them sitting there on the curb and went to find the temple groundskeeper. I found him in the powerhouse with a hammer in his hand.

"Go to the front of the temple." I whispered. He stopped what he was doing, wondering what brought that thought to his mind. When he continued with his work, I repeated, this time a little louder, "Go to the front of the temple." His reception was good. I could see that he was used to following his thoughts when spoken to. He lay down his hammer and took off along the sidewalk. When he turned the corner he saw two little girls sitting on the curb. As he approached they turned to look at him, waiting to see what this man wanted to say. He said nothing, just looked at them. He decided that they looked like two innocent little girls just sitting there talking. Nothing seemed to be amiss, so he smiled at them and turned to go back to work. He knew that sometimes a thought could be your own thought and not one given by an angel like me. Believing that it had been his own thought, he turned to go back to what he was doing.

"Why are they sitting here at the temple?" I prompted him. There was that thought again, so he turned back and asked, "What are you girls doing here?"

Sally spoke right up and told him about her friends in the temple and that she could not go with them.

I whispered, "Mister, you can take them to see the font."

The groundskeeper caught on right away, as usual, and told them to wait. He would get permission to show them around. Soon other people came, and the girls were escorted around the block to the powerhouse, through the powerhouse, along a secret tunnel under the beautiful lawn and trees, and into the basement of the temple.

Right there, above them, was the bottom of a big, brownish-looking bowl. The groundskeeper pointed to it and said, "That is the bottom of the font." Sally looked straight up at that round bowl. He continued, "Your friends are right up there above you."

"Oh, that would be so wonderful." I saw a tear appear in Sally's eye. As she blinked, it rolled down her cheek. Now she was close to her friends and close to where the baptisms were being done. I tuned into her thoughts: "Will I ever be able to go there? Will I ever be part of their church and their Primary?"

"Be patient," I comforted her. "Someday you will. I promise."

Sally smiled. There was a new light in her face. She could wait.

At age twenty-four, a grown girl was standing at the edge of the baptismal font in the very same temple where she had waited on the curb many years ago. She still had dark brown curly hair. The ringlets had now changed to beautiful natural curls that still clung snugly to her neck.

I knew who she was and why she was standing there. Now dressed in white, she was ready for the baptism that she had longed for long ago.

As she stood there, it was not the beautiful clear water she was looking at, nor was it the twelve strong oxen circling the font, but it was the little girl she remembered from so long ago, standing below looking up at her. They were one and the same. Both had dark brown curly hair framing the light that shone in their faces. She had longed for this day, and now her longing had come true.

"Thank you, R^2," she thought. "Thank you for remembering me and for keeping your promise."

"You are very welcome, my dear Sally," I whispered. Then I clipped a brown curl from her neck.

I did it. How could I? I actually did it. One of her curly brown locks was resting softly in my hand. I could feel it. How could this be? As an angel, I have never experienced anything like this. What happened?

Then someone whispered to me, "R^2, love accomplishes miracles."

"Oh my . . ." Sally had left her mark on me.

A little green house
Inviting . . . Open the door
Forest of two-by-fours

The Little Green House

Positive vibes from a little green house on Northline Lane caught my attention, so I dropped into a forest of two-by-fours. Yes, two-by-fours. The little green house was neat and painted on the outside, yet unfinished on the inside. Laughing children were playing, racing from room to room through the walls with the dog hot at their heels and the calico cat observing from the windowsill. Who needs a door in this wide open home? The dirt from the mother's broom was falling through the knotholes in the bare floor boards, and the father was nailing some boxes on the kitchen wall for the dishes. Large unfolded cardboard boxes lay on the floor, ready to be nailed up as walls for privacy. Smiles and happy sounds were everywhere. This was their own new home, and they were happy.

This little family had just moved in, changing this little house to a home. Renting was no more. Through a family council, the decision was made to purchase this little green house and finish the inside with the money that would have gone for rent. Luckily it was summertime; the sky was blue, and the sun was warm. Up the lane was the Trans-Canada Highway 1. Across the lane was a pool of runoff water from the rain, the home of water snakes and frogs. Down at the end of the lane was a forest of trees as numerous as the two-by-fours. Hidden in the forest of trees was a pig farm. Oink!

The sad little unfinished green house had been on the market for a long time, but now it was a happy little unfinished green house because it had been chosen to be a home. Looking through the two-by-fours I could see a bed and a dresser in one bedroom for Jennie and little Lisa and a bunk bed and a dresser in the other bedroom for Matt and Tommy. In the bathroom there were no utilities, only unpacked boxes, but there was a new outhouse in the backyard. In the kitchen under the window, there was one pipe sticking up through the floor. This pipe had one tap for running cold water. A newfangled stove had been moved into the kitchen—one that used some kind of sawdust that continually burned if you kept the bin filled. This big, heavy, square stove was used for cooking, for heating water, and for warmth. A big chesterfield[1] bed where the parents slept sat along one wall in the living room. The living room also contained a TV and a big, soft chair. The washer was in the back entry. The dryer consisted of several lines strung up in the backyard. This was home.

Max, the father, called to his wife, "Honey, would you please come see if you can reach the top of this box for your dishes."

Susie, the mother, dropped her broom and reached up. "Just barely," she said. "That height will be okay." She held the box while he finished driving the nails into the two-by-fours. "How many boxes did you get?"

"I was lucky to get six of them. Three of them will be

end to end at this height and then I will put three more under them."

"I will make curtains to hang over the boxes to keep the dishes clean," she said. "Until the floor is finished there will be a lot of dust flying around." She turned back to her broom and Max stooped to pick up another box.

I spoke to Max, "That is quite a wife you have there."

Max stopped and looked at his wife, the box still in his hand.

"Do you love her?" I asked.

"Of course I love her." He watched her sweep the dirt in a neat little pile and then nudge it down a knothole.

"She is a good sport to move into a place like this," I added.

"I adore her for being such a good sport."

"Do you ever tell her that?"

"I think that she just knows."

"A little hug and a squeeze sometimes will confirm it for her, you know."

Max put the box back down, walked up behind Susie, and put his arms around her. She looked sideways at him with a cute grin and said, "What are you doing?" She slipped around in his arms to face him. It felt so warm.

"When I saw you edging that dirt into that little hole a strange feeling came over me. Are you sure you want to go through with this?"

"Of course. We agreed on it."

"I mean, really, do you want to do this? It is not very fancy for the woman I love."

"We will make it fancy. It will be an adventure to experience every step of the way. Every little improvement will be like a miracle before our eyes. A miracle that we make happen."

"You are such a good sport, and I love you."

She lay her head on his chest, knowing that this would be a challenge for both of them. She vowed to herself that she would give him all her support. He was such a good man, and she loved him dearly. The tender moment was broken with a crash as they were clipped by the dog taking a shortcut to catch the children. She would have fallen had he not held her tight. They both laughed.

Then the cat fell apart. It had moved to a box under the stove. I noticed that she was a "fat cat"—but not that kind of fat. Susie heard a little meow and when she checked it out, Mimi had a new kitten in her box. Susie quickly called the children. As they came running, she shushed them and said, "Be very quiet. Look what Mimi has." There was silence, with a few tender oohs and aahs. They all kneeled down on the floor by the box, including Max—and me. It had been a long time since I had witnessed such a miracle.

"It is a little tabby," Max said.

"What's a tabby?" quizzed Lisa.

"Tabby's are usually gray with little dark gray stripes." The children watched it nose around its mother's tummy, looking for milk.

"It can't see where to go," said Tommy. "Its eyes are not open."

"It takes a few days before they open their eyes," said Mother. Just then another little head appeared and the children held their breath as another kitten was born.

I whispered to Susie, "This is a very important teaching moment for your children." She caught on right away, wondering what to tell them about birthing. She watched their faces for clues.

"Look!" Jennie was excited. "This one is spotted."

"It is a calico. It looks like its mother," commented big brother Matt.

"That's right, Matt," Max said, "It is the same with us. Some of you children look like me, and some of you look like Mom."

I watched the children as they started looking at each other and then at their Mom and Dad, trying to find the resemblance. During this time Mimi's tongue was very busy, licking and licking the new kittens to get them clean and dry.

Susie continued teaching. "I think that calico cats are usually girl cats. I read in the encyclopedia that calico cats can be a boy cat, but that a calico boy cat cannot reproduce."

"What does reproduce mean?"

"Reproduce means that it cannot be a daddy cat. It is only a cat. Girl cats can be mother cats and boy cats can be daddy cats, but calico boy cats cannot be a daddy cat."

"I hope that this one is a girl cat."

"What should we name them?" asked Lisa.

Max spoke up, "How about Eeny for the first one and Meeny for the second one?" The children caught on right away and giggled as they thought of the nursery rhyme.

"Can I pick up Eeny, Mom? It is all dry," asked little Tommy.

"No, we must not touch them yet; it might make the mother nervous."

"Oh," he mumbled, "it is so cute."

"Look, here comes another one," Jennie called out.

"It's orange. Miney is orange." The new name came automatically.

"I had an orange cat for a pet one time when I was young," Susie said. "Someone told me that all orange cats are boy cats; at least mine was a boy. I am not sure, but that is what I heard." Then mother added. "When I was a girl on the ranch, we had lots of cats in the barn. My dad liked them there because they kept the barn clean by killing the mice."

I could see that mother was really in a storytelling-mode now, remembering the wild cats in her family barn.

"My sister and I would try to catch them for pets. We would search all through the hay where they hid and try to corner them. They could really scratch and bite, and they would hiss at us when we got near."

"How did you dare you pick them up then?"

"Very carefully. We would put on our dad's big gloves and then grab with both hands at the same time. One hand would grab the back of the neck and the other hand the tail. This way we could stretch them out so they couldn't scratch or bite."

"Did that hurt them?"

"No, we were careful. But if we missed with one hand, we had to drop them in a hurry because they were fast. We got lots of scratches, but it was fun."

Matt shouted, "Here comes Moe. It is *way* spotted—more spotted than Meeny. It looks more like its mother than Meeny does."

"Now we have two girls," beamed Jennie, making use of the knowledge she had just acquired.

"That is the end of our rhyme," the children chorused. "We have Eeny, Meeny, Miney, and Moe. Mimi must be finished having kittens. . . . but wait, here is another one."

"What should we name it?" They were puzzled.

I whispered to Matt, "This is the last one—there are no more."

So Matt spoke up and said, "Let's call the last one Nomore." I laughed. Matt got my prompting and wittily named the last kitten. Everyone laughed. The children continued saying Nomore, Nomore, Nomore so many times that it ended up sounding like Nomoe. That fit in perfectly: Eeny, Meeny, Miney, Moe, and Nomoe. Nomoe was a tabby too.

Soon all the five kittens were clean and dry—all lined up eating.

"Mom, are they eating their mother?" Tommy asked.

"No. See the little nipples? That is where the babies drink their milk." Mimi allowed them to check out the little nipples and then Susie added, "The kittens are all busy now, so the class is over for today."

The children went back to their games, chanting Eeny, Meeny, Miney, Moe, and Nomoe.

Susie ran her hand over Mimi's warm, colorful body, acknowledging the monumental task she had just witnessed. She gently stroked her soft hair a few more times. Mimi looked up. Their eyes met in understanding. Then the box was gently pushed back under the stove where it was warm and private.

Another day meant another improvement. Max was a real handyman: a carpenter, a plumber, an everything. The cardboard boxes were up, new plywood and linoleum covered all the floors, new warm rugs lay by the bedsides, and the new kitchen cupboards were nearly finished. The dishes were scattered on the shelves where Max was not working. There was warm and cold water in the sink taps. I heard Susie say that was like heaven. When not helping and holding things for Max, she had made curtains for the windows. Her home was beginning to look as fancy as Max had promised.

One important thing had not happened yet. The bathroom space was still storage space. The new outhouse in the backyard still took care of that chore. "Max," I said, "when are you going to finish the bathroom?"

I saw the disappointment on Susie's face. She had always had a bathroom inside. This is the one thing she was embarrassed about in their new home. She could handle the holey floors, the cardboard walls, and the boxes for cupboards, but she could not handle the outhouse.

"Susie," I whispered. "Let's dress up the outhouse."

"Dress up the outhouse? I want to dress up the bathroom."

"The outhouse could really be the talk of the town."

"Oh, it already is the talk of the town."

"I will help you. It could be a project between the two of us."

"R^2, that sounds silly."

I touched her shoulder, just slightly, to let her know I was there. "First, we will whitewash the whole inside. Then we will stick up some pretty wallpaper." Susie could see it all in her mind, and she was forming ideas of her own.

"We could put real hinged seats on the holes."

"Yes!"

"It needs a new name instead of outhouse."

"When I was a child, we called it a Biffy."

"Biffy?"

"Yes, that's old Canadian slang for a toilet or bathroom."

"I love it! Biffy it is." She even put up a sign.

When Susie hung up a nice roll of toilet paper, I spoke up. "Susie, you need a catalog in there."

"A catalog?"

I could tell she was confused. "Yes, a catalog. It goes with the Biffy territory—makes it more authentic. You take last year's Eaton's catalog, drill a hole in one corner, insert a string, and loop the string over a nail."

"Catalog paper is not very soft."

"Don't you know the technique to make it soft?" Susie shook her head, so I explained. "As soon as you sit down, you tear a page out of the catalog then crinkle it up, straighten it out, crinkle it up, straighten it out, crinkle it up, straighten it out. Continue this process so that by the time you are ready to use it, it is soft."

"You're kidding." She laughed.

"Works every time. Something else that works well is the soft papers that fruit used to be wrapped in. Our apples always came in a box, with each apple carefully wrapped individually. I should warn you, though—don't let anyone put peach papers in there." Susie looked puzzled, and I added, "You could itch for a week."

"Yow," she screeched. "R^2, you are so much fun."

The pond and the forest were the favorite places for the children to play. The pond was just deep enough to come to the top of their gum boots. Susie bought the children high rubber boots so they would keep their feet dry. Somehow they still got their feet wet. The challenge was to see how deep they could go to catch the frogs and water snakes. Lisa would scream and run when the boys chased her with the snakes. Jennie didn't scream because she was one of the chasers.

I looked when I heard a yowl, and I saw their little kitten Moe in the pond, so I hurried to tell Jennie. "Find Moe!" I shouted. Jennie heard my strong prompting and remembered that she had put Moe down when she found a snake.

"You had better check," I warned.

Jennie hurried back and there was Moe in water over her head. Jennie picked up the wet, limp kitten and ran to the little green house yelling at the top of her voice, "Mom, Mom, Moe has drowned. I found her in the water."

"Oh, no," Susie moaned as she wrapped Moe in a

towel and held her close to warm her. The neighborhood children had heard Jennie yelling and all gathered to see the water-soaked kitten. All their faces looked tense and worried for little Moe.

"Susie," I whispered, "Moe is still alive." Susie looked closer and thought she saw a little ear twitch.

"Get some air into her," I called. "You know CPR." Immediately Susie started breathing into the little mouth and nose, then she squeezed Moe a little and then gave her breath again. This process went on for a few seconds until Susie felt Moe's small wet body start to move a little.

"Susie," I continued, "Remember the whiskey your Dad would give to the little lambs when they were so cold and near death?" She remembered seeing the limp little lambs brought into the house and put in a box behind the warm stove.

"Does anyone here have any whiskey at your home?" she asked the children.

"We do," shouted one girl.

"Run and get it. Quick." Off she ran and soon returned with the whole bottle.

"Someone get a spoon," Susie called, and soon a spoon appeared with a few drops of whiskey in it. Susie opened Moe's mouth gently and slid a drop in. It must have been strong because within seconds Moe gave a big body twist, and a screeching m-e-o-w swooshed from her mouth. It must have vibrated clear down to the forest. Finally, when Moe settled down, Susie gently put her in the cat box under the warm stove. One drop had reminded her little heart what it was there for. Moe lived, just as the little lambs had lived. But at times Moe would sway sideways, and the children would help her get on her feet again. She became a very special pet.

And then there was the forest. It was the favorite place

for the neighborhood children to play. One day as they played, I noticed five-year-old Lisa was not with the children. I spied her in the far corner of the trees, going the wrong way. I called to her, "Lisa, Lisa." She was crying, and she wouldn't tune in. "Lisa, turn around and go the other way." There was no response. I followed her. She could see a fence in the distance and headed for it. There were no trees inside the fence; it was all bare and muddy. Lisa started to crawl through the fence. "Don't," I called. She just kept climbing through and crying. Her tears made rivulets down her dirty face. Her foot got caught, and she fell in the mud. I tried to pick her up, but of course I couldn't. "Get up, Lisa," I called. Her crying caught the attention of the pigs. Yes, she was in the pigpen in the forest. They came running to her. I tried to shoo them away, but again I had no power to do that. I tried to protect her from them; no luck. The pen was getting sloppier with mud so deep that her gum boots were getting stuck. She fell and then struggled to get up, but the mud seemed to hold tight. Of course, the pigs were curious and approached her with their pink snouts for a whiff. There were big pigs, small pigs, spotted pigs, black pigs, red pigs, long snouts, short snouts, droopy ears, and erect ears; all grunted in wonderment. Now Lisa was screaming, screaming, screaming. Some of the pigs squealed and ran around, frightened. They backed off, making a circle around her. Every way she looked there were pigs, pigs, pigs looking at her. She finally got up on her feet again but couldn't walk as the mud sucked her gum boots right down to hard ground. What a pitiful sight!

 I rushed back to the little green house to Susie. I shouted, "Lisa is in trouble!" As the thought came to Lisa's mother, she stopped still. I repeated it, a little stronger. "Lisa is in trouble." Susie took off on a run for the forest.

I hurried back to Lisa and then saw the farmer in his yard. Rushing to him, I called, "Come quick, a little girl is stuck in your pigpen."

The farmer got a puzzled look on his face. "A little girl in my pigpen?" he mumbled. "What is a little girl doing in my pigpen?" He wondered where the thought came from.

I called to him again. "Come quick, come quick." This time he looked toward the pigpen and saw the pigs all standing in a circle.

"That is weird," he thought. Then I noticed that the farmer was squinting and realized that he had lost one eye. Finally, when he did see Lisa, he ran and picked her up and carried her out of the pen. What a sight! She had forest mud and pigpen mud all over her while muddy teardrops dripped off her chin. The crying had stopped now, but quiet sobs still shook her little body. She felt safe in this man's arms.

Susie came and took her home. She washed Lisa off with the hose, took off the soggy clothes, and put her in the old round tub filled with warm water. What a fright that had been!

I enjoyed helping children because they were so receptive to my counsel. At least most of them were. I found that the boy who lived in the back of the corner store at Trans-Canada Highway and Northline Lane would not listen to me. He was Billy, the neighborhood bully. No matter how I tried, he never responded to me. Once he had some candy but would not share it with anyone. He just teased and ate it in front of them. Another time he shared it with one person while the rest stood by, feeling weird. If he found a child alone, he would threaten them, push them around, and send them home crying. Several times the children from the little green house were victims. I finally talked to the boys and asked, "Are you afraid of Billy?"

"Yes, he is bigger than us," they answered.

"Is he bigger than the both of you together?"

"No, but he hits real hard."

"So he hits one of you hard, and you both run. Is that right?"

"Yes."

"I think that you could scare him if you teamed up on him."

"What do you mean?"

"If he pushes one of you, get together and push him back."

"We wouldn't dare to do that." I could see the fright in their eyes.

"But it would scare him if you did it together. Do you want him to stop scaring you?"

"Yes."

"Then you have to stick together. Now listen to this because it is very important. Do not cause a fight. Your mother has told you it is not good to fight, and she is right. But you need to stick up for yourself and protect each other when there is trouble." I could see their minds working on the possibility of such an idea.

They took off up the lane to Billy's store. I followed them. When Billy saw them coming, he walked to meet them. The boys' next few steps slowed down. "Keep going," I encouraged. "Pass right by him as if he wasn't there." As they passed, Billy reached out and shoved Tommy because Tommy was the smallest one. Both boys turned around and shoved him back. Billy was surprised. He was not used to this. Billy stepped toward them again, and again both boys pushed him. It took a lot of courage, but they did it.

"Keep walking now," I told them. They continued on to the store. They had no reason to go into the store, so they stopped and wondered what to do. "Just walk back home now as if nothing had happened," I coached. They did. When they passed Billy, they could see that he was eyeing them closely for more pushes. He did not push. Neither did they. They just walked on by.

"That was pretty easy," they agreed.

"You boys were great," I complimented them, and they smiled, so I continued. "Let me give another suggestion—for the next few times you see Billy, always be together. I think that he will try to make friends with you. Did you know that a bully is usually a coward, so he gets quarrelsome and picks on smaller people. He likes to make people think he is brave when he really isn't. He can be a good friend though if you try."

When I spoke to Billy this time, he humbly listened. "Those boys could be your good friends, Billy. Do you know that?"

Billy understood, and they did become good friends, even on a one-to-one basis.

Then Max got a call from his nineteen-year-old cousin, Bert, who was calling from the food line in Vancouver.

"What's up, Bert?" he asked.

"Things aren't going so well—thought I might come to see . . ."

"Tell me where you are, and I will be right there."

Max and I picked him up and brought him home with us. He was so hungry that he ate an entire loaf of bread with jam while Susie cooked his dinner. I have never seen anyone eat so enthusiastically.

"Bert is our cousin," Max told the children as they looked on in amazement. They were very quiet. He looked kind of scary.

"He has no hair," Lisa whispered to Jennie.

"Shhhh," was the answer.

Bert heard the whisper and smiled at Lisa. "Do you know that I can wash my hair with a face cloth?" Lisa hid behind Jennie while the rest laughed.

Max continued, "Bert has been in Vancouver and has been trying to find a job." Then he turned to Bert. "Would you like to stay with us until you find a job?"

Bert glanced at Susie and then back at Max. "Sure, but . . ." Bert could see that it was a small house with lots of sleepers. Max looked at Susie, and she kind of shrugged, knowing that all the beds were full, but how could they say no?

"Max," I suggested, "the bathroom."

Max's gaze went that way. "How about the bathroom, Bert?" he said with a laugh. Everyone laughed and moved to the little storage room. The look on Bert's face told them that he was surprised that this family did not have an inside bathroom.

"Our Biffy is behind the house," chirped Tommy.

"Biffy?" asked Bert.

"An *outhouse!*" Tommy yelled. "We call it a Biffy." Susie gasped and wondered what Bert would think about that.

"We had an outhouse when I was a kid," said Bert, trying to ease Susie's mind. "We had lots of fun with it. When my sister would go in there, I would throw rocks at the outhouse—I mean, the Biffy—and my sister would get mad at me because it would scare her and make her jump. It was fun to tease her."

"Our Biffy is special because we have flowered wall paper inside and pretty flowers growing outside," boasted Jennie.

Max got out his measuring tape—measured the length

of the boy's bunk bed and then measured the length of the bathroom. "Perfect fit," he said. He and Bert took off to the Army and Navy store while Susie and the children moved the storage boxes into the bedrooms.

Soon an old army bunk bed with angle-iron posts, two mattresses, and an old dresser were fitted in that little room. Susie hung an unused bed sheet over the door for privacy and Bert had his own private room. He laughed and said it reminded him of what his own grandpa always said: "There is not enough room in there to cuss out a cat without getting hair in your mouth." All joined Bert in his laugh.

Two days later, Bert got a job at a nearby box factory, and Susie had a boarder in her bathroom. Days were fun as Bert fit in "right good."

Then one day we had a good laugh when Bert asked, "Susie, would you mind if I bought some tea? I noticed that you do not use it, but I like to drink tea sometimes."

"I have some tea in my cupboard." Susie answered. "I keep it there for my father when he comes to visit us. He likes tea. You may use it if you like."

So Bert made his own tea. The children got a kick out of watching Bert drink his tea. If it was too hot, he would pour some of it in his saucer and hold the saucer with three fingers, pointer finger on the top and thumb and middle finger under the rim of the saucer. Then he would sip. It was quite a skill.

Once when their kitten Moe meowed at his feet, Bert put some tea in his saucer and set it down for the kitten to drink. We all laughed when we saw the kitten sniff it and turn around and try to cover her nose with her little paw. We knew what Moe thought of the tea, and the laugh was on Bert.

A month later Bert came home with a new friend who

had just been hired at the box factory. Bert asked, "He does not have a place to stay. Susie, could he sleep in the top bunk?"

Now Susie had two boarders in her bathroom.

As Bert and his friend worked and saved their money, they soon moved into their own apartment. Using the saved room and board money, Max and Susie got the little green house a new swanky bathroom. If fancy flowered Biffies could be sad, I think this one was.

I enjoyed my stay with this family in the little green house. They lived together, worked together, loved together, learned together, played together, and grew together. No matter what hardships and inconveniences they experienced, they made it an adventure to remember. Susie got her fancy home because it was a happy home. They were very pleased, and so was I.

Then Max got a promotion. The little green house was sold. California sounded wonderful to the children, but Susie cried.

"Susie," I whispered to her. "Susie, you have really loved this home, haven't you?"

"Yes, R^2, I really have. My whole heart and soul are built into this little green house."

I warmly touched her shoulder, and I could tell she knew that I was there. "Look around," I said as I guided her thoughts. She remembered the forest of two-by-fours, the knotholes in the floor, and the boxes on the wall full of dishes. She could still see flattened cardboard boxes on the walls. When she saw the chesterfield, she laughed and said, "I always looked forward to the day when I would not have to be a guest in my own home and would not have to sleep in the living room any more. Now the chesterfield is sold and gone with all the rest."

"You will have new stuff in California."

"I dreamed of California, but now I wonder about that."

We walked to the newly finished bathroom. A little sob tore at her. Then we walked out the back door to the Biffy.

She pointed. "That was your idea, R^2. We loved to show that off to the neighbors. Will it get all dusty and full of spiderwebs now?" Another sob. We walked back into the house. I stepped back as Max came in and found Susie crying. He held her tight for a long time, until the sobs eased. Then he wiped her face and gently kissed her forehead. "Are you sorry we're going?"

"No, no. It is good to move on. But I have loved this little house so much."

"We know every inch of it, don't we?"

"Yes, we found it full of two-by-fours, lonesome and bare, and we made it into a lovely, happy home."

"Do you think it has any feelings? What a story it could tell."

They walked out hand in hand. Max closed the door. Susie turned her head away as she heard him turn the key. The family drove up the dusty lane and away.

Yes, Max, what a story it could tell. And now the story has been told. It is a resplendent story of love, hardship, sharing, laughing, and gratitude. I was so touched by this family that I placed my R^2 above the front door of the little green house and the moon on the Biffy. The new owners will feel the spirit of this family as soon as they step in the door. I promise. —R^2

> *One mortal blossom*
> *Returning to its home? Aah!*
> *A white butterfly*

Something Grabbed My Pen

Something grabbed Grace's pen and wrote, "Your mother wants her temple work done as soon as possible." The pen was flying and the words came so fast that Grace could hardly hold onto the pen.

I, R^2, had this special message for Grace. Actually, the message was not from me, but I was assigned to get her to pray so she could receive her special message. I was having a hard time getting through to her. She was a new member of The Church of Jesus Christ of Latter-day Saints and had not recognized the whisperings of the still small voice, which was me.

Grace's mother had been a member long ago but had forgotten. She had even forgotten to teach her children the beauties of the gospel. Grace found it on her own through a nice young man who taught her the gospel and then married her. Grace was so excited that she wanted her brother to know of the Church. They were baptized together.

When Grace's mother became very ill, she realized

that her time on this earth might be short, and she had not gone to the temple for these blessings.

I had nudged the mother's conscience and whispered to her, "Do you remember when you were baptized?"

"Oh, yes," she remembered. "I turned eight years old on March 19 and was baptized on April 9. Oh, it was soooo cold. Some ice was still clinging to the edge of the St. Mary's River. They broke it away for my baptism. I shall never forget it." She shuddered just thinking about it.

I quizzed her more, "Did you go to church?"

"No." She paused. I could hear a depressed tone in her voice. "I should have. After I was married I didn't go to church. I found it easier to stay at home with my husband, who was not a member."

"How about your children?"

"They didn't go either." This time she paused a long time. "For that I am so sorry." I could see that she was truly repentant. I could also see that she realized that it was too late now—the time had passed, and the children were gone.

Another quiz. "Did you go to the temple?"

Complete silence.

"You can still get your temple blessing, you know," I whispered to her in a positive tone.

"But how could I do that? I can hardly get out of bed. My heart is acting strangely, and I have such a hard time breathing."

"Your daughter Grace has found the LDS Church on her own and is a member now."

"I know. I'm so pleased about that."

"Do you know that she can do the temple ordinances for you?"

"Oh, yes, I remember about that proxy business. That will be after I am gone."

"Yes, after you are gone one year. That is one of the rules in doing temple blessings. So ask her," I encouraged.

The mother did ask her daughter, and Grace made a promise that the work would be done.

Now the year was up and Grace had forgotten. I, R^2, had been given the mission to remind her.

I found Grace practicing songs on the piano. She had several children ready to take piano lessons. After some calculations, she decided that it would be cheaper if she took the lessons herself and then taught her own children. She rented a piano, bought some beginning books, and got started. It was working very well. The older children were starting to play so well that Grace could hardly keep ahead of them. One day Grace's neighbor asked her if she would teach her child piano lessons. Grace was surprised. "I am not a teacher," she replied.

"Oh, but you are a teacher," she praised. "Look how well your children play." So Grace agreed to teach the neighbor's child. She charged two dollars per lesson. The ripple effect from that one child brought thirty. Grace soon had a brand new "two dollar" piano. Recitals were held; parents were pleased. Grace found, though, that when her students got to the second-grade levels in playing, she needed to send them off to more advanced teachers.

It was while Grace was playing the piano that I made my first contact. I let my presence be felt by allowing a warm feeling to be present. She felt it right away. She had been a member of the LDS Church only a short time, yet she recognized this as something spiritual.

"I wonder what is wanted of me," she thought. "Maybe I am supposed to be better at the piano. Maybe I am supposed to serve others by playing the piano." This inspiration caused Grace to be at the piano as much as she could, practicing and practicing, teaching and teaching. It reminded her of her mother, who was a very good ragtime piano player. Her mother also chorded on the piano to accompany her dad's fiddle at the old time dances. Her dad had owned the dance hall in Kimball.

"Yes, my mother would be happy that I am playing the piano," Grace said to herself, so she continued to play and practice every time she could.

The piano playing impression *did* remind her of her mother, but it was her temple blessings that I needed her to think of, not the piano. This was not working; she was getting the wrong message. I tried to contact her several times the next week or so, but my presence seemed to make her play the piano all the more.

I realized I must try something to get her off that piano thing.

Next I caught her chopping some kindling in the backyard. She cooked on a wood and coal stove and was pretty handy at chopping her kindling to make her fire. I thought I had an idea that would work..

I made sure that she felt my same presence again. She dropped the little hatchet and stood in amazement; there was such a puzzled look was on her face.

"Yoo-hoo," I shouted. That worked.

"What is going on?" she questioned. "Surely I am not supposed to chop wood the rest of my life." She gave a fierce "humph" and jerked her arm down with fists doubled. She picked up her little pile of kindling and went back into the house still in a daze.

"Tell your husband," I whispered.

"I have been telling him. I told him about the piano, and he agreed that I should do as I am inspired to do. Now if I tell him about this kindling stuff, he will laugh at me."

"Well, I am laughing too, but it worked, didn't it?"

"I will not stop playing the piano," she told me in no uncertain terms. I could tell she was disgusted with me.

"Now, as I said before, go tell your husband."

She did tell her husband. Being wise and understanding, he didn't laugh. He told her that she must pray about it.

"Oh, no," she gasped. "I cannot pray about it."

"Why not?"

"Because I am afraid of what might happen."

"What could happen?"

"I am not ready to see any bodies." This time he did laugh.

He knew that she was a new member of the church. He knew also that she had a very strong testimony about visions, and she wasn't ready for anything like that.

She did not pray. I kept bugging her about it.

Finally Grace asked her husband, "Will you pray for me?" she begged. "You know a lot more about praying than I do." He tried to explain that it was she, herself, who must ask.

She did not pray. I continued to bug her. Several weeks passed and still no praying.

Next she begged her husband to go with her and hold her hand while she prayed. He stood firm, yet gently encouraged her, "You can do it."

Another week went by, and I made contact with her often, nearly every day, but she wouldn't follow her husband's advice. He had told her that it was through prayer that she needed to receive the message.

She did not pray. She was beginning to feel guilty for not praying. In fact, she had started missing her daily prayers because of it. She was conscious of her husband's questioning eyes.

Finally one evening, she decided she was ready. The children were all tucked snug in bed, and her husband was reading. Grace went to her husband and picked up his hand for a moment. He put down the paper and looked questioningly at her. Her eyes told him what she was ready to do. Then she disappeared into her bedroom, alone. It was dark in there except for a slight light shining from the next room. She knelt to pray.

Nothing happened. She prayed for quite a long time. Nothing happened. When she came out of the bedroom, her husband's eyes questioned her for a moment and then he softly asked, "Well?"

"Nothing." She looked puzzled. He folded his arms around her and held her close. Grace relaxed in his arms.

"Any answer as to what is wanted?" he asked.

"No." She shook her head and seemed confused, so he continued to hold her in his arms.

Again he asked, "Anything unusual come to your mind?"

Grace thought for a while and then softly said to him, "Well, there was one thought—Mom's temple work."

"That's it." He called out, jumping back and flinging his arms in the air. "That's it." He was excited. At once he had the problem solved. "Write a letter to your brother and his wife. They live close to a temple; they can do it."

Grace picked up a pen to write—and something grabbed her pen.

So there it goes. *I* did it. *She* did it. *We* did it. I felt like dancing. The message finally got through.

The brother wrote back with the following message: "I am sure that Mother chose *you* to do her temple work as she had asked you a year ago. Please come visit us." So Grace was able to carry out her promise to her mother in the Salt Lake Temple.

However, there was one disappointment. Grace was sure that her mother would be at the temple—maybe she would hear her voice or even see her. Grace had heard stories about that happening, but neither one did. Grace found an empty room and had a good cry. Her husband found her, wiped her tears, held her close, and said with assurance, "Your mother has had the permission to contact you. Now you can be assured that she has accepted the work and is happily on her way. You have released her to continue on with whatever she has been assigned to do."

Mother and daughter are now connected for eternity. It is a good feeling to be connected.

It takes a lot of creativity for the Spirit to guide you where to go, to tell you what to do, or to answer your questions. Grace and I often laugh about all the shenanigans I went through to get my message through to her. That's my job!

Now every time Grace goes to the temple, she sees my R^2 on the angel and, I hope, thinks of me. —R^2

Break law of nature
Penitence of one's own guilt
Brings closure

The Last Chicken

I followed a lady into the butcher shop. It was an old-fashioned butcher shop where the chickens and roasts and such were all kept in wooden barrels. It was late in the day, and the lady hoped that there would be a chicken left for her.

"Do you have any chickens left? I am sorry that I am so late. Your chickens are probably gone."

"Let me check," the butcher answered. I could see in the chicken barrel; there was only one left. The butcher picked up that last chicken and put it on the scale.

"How much does it weigh?" she asked.

"It is just three and one-half pounds," he read.

"Do you have any a little bigger?" she asked. "I would like more than three and one-half pounds."

"I'll check." The butcher walked back to the barrel, put the chicken in and then picked up the same chicken again.

"Uh oh," I thought. "What is he up to?"

I watched as he put that same chicken on the scale

and then, along with some thumb pressure behind the chicken, he said, "This one is four pounds. Would you like this one?"

I hurried over to the lady and whispered loudly in her ear, "Take both chickens."

"Yes," replied the lady. "I will take both of them."

The butcher hemmed and hawed and finally said, "Well... I was saving the four pound chicken for my wife. I promised her that I would bring one home tonight."

"Hey, butcher," I teased. "You are caught."

He looked sheepish. I was glad that he felt guilty.

"Hey, butcher," I said again in an accusing tone. "Do you do that thumb trick to all your customers? For shame!" Then I had an idea. "If you are sorry—really sorry," I told him, "give her the chicken."

The surprised shopper went home with her chicken, compliments of the butcher... and me.

My R^2 was placed on the heavy thumb of the butcher as a reminder. He was not a happy butcher, but I smiled and even had the last laugh.—R^2

Glorious heaven
Pierced by the spires of love
Ha! It's a temple

Be Still and Listen

I was there when Rachel received a phone call. "Rachel, I have a favor to ask of you." It was Judy, mother of Rhet, my favorite nephew.

"Sure," Rachel replied, "What can I do for you?"

"Did you know that Rhet is going on a mission for the Church?"

"Yes. You told me that when he got his call to Kentucky."

"Well, he is going to the temple for the first time next Tuesday."

"That is wonderful, Judy."

"Now here is my favor; would you come with us?"

"You know I would love to."

"Rhet chose you to go with us as you are his favorite aunt."

"And his only aunt." They laughed. Then she added, "Tell Rhet that I am so honored."

Tuesday had arrived, so I reminded Rachel, "Today is the day for you to go to the temple with Rhet and his parents." She didn't need much reminding; she has been thinking about it all week. She even took the day off from work.

"Don't forget to take your temple recommend," I reminded her. She knew, as I know, that one must have a recommend from the bishop in order to enter the temple. Many people are not aware of that.

I remember being present when a lady from one of the embassies in Washington, D.C., found that out. Her name was Betty. As she was being driven on the North Beltway that circles the city, they rounded a corner and there, to her wonderment, a fairy princess castle seemed to rise up in front of the road.

She gasped. "What is that?"

"I don't know," replied her driver.

"Find it!" she ordered. After getting off the freeway, they wandered around in the Kensington area, where beautiful trees hid the streets as well as the horizon. Finally there it was, surrounded by colorful, blossoming trees. She took in the whole scene: the sign said, "Washington Temple, The Church of Jesus Christ of Latter-day Saints"; six pointed temple towers pierced the heavenly sky; and a golden angel, standing atop the highest peak, pressed a golden trumpet to his lips.

She was breathless. It was a resplendent moment. "Stop the car."

"Yes, Miss Betty," the driver replied as he pulled up into the overhead drive and helped her out. She disappeared into the big doors.

"May I help you?" asked a lady dressed in all white.

Betty was aglow. "What a beautiful building," she told the lady. "May I have a tour?"

"Yes, we have a tour of the lobby and of the surrounding grounds."

"I mean a tour inside this beautiful building," she exclaimed passionately.

"I am sorry, but we do not have tours inside of the temple. However," she added, "I suggest that you go inquire at the visitors' center. They can help you. The visitors' center is the building just north of here."

I could see the disappointment in Betty's face and actions, yet she politely gave her thanks and disappeared back through the big doors.

The next stop was the visitors' center, where Betty met the director, who looked very professional in his suit and tie. He listened to her story and offered to show her around the center. "You see," he explained to her, "because you are from one of the embassies, you are a political visitor to our country; therefore, we are not allowed to preach the gospel of Jesus Christ to you. We can, however, tell you that the Church is worldwide. We can also tell you about the people in the Church: they are obedient to the laws of the land in which they live, they are good and industrious, and they love their families."

I, as an angel, must put my own words of explanation in here. I call this fat-free proselyting.

The visitors' center director took Betty on a little tour and then said, "If you want to know more about the Church, I suggest you go to the International Affairs Office. It is located in the National Press Building on Fourteenth and F Streets."

Betty was on a hunt and wasn't about to give up. Soon she was sitting across the desk from the director of the International Affairs Office. After the pleasantries were exchanged, Betty asked about the beautiful temple that took her breath away. It was explained to her that only people who are good members of the Church are allowed to enter the temple.

Angels Have the Last Laugh

"Well, I don't know anything about your church except what I have heard today," was her comment. "I think I would like to know more, but it seems to me that no one can tell me more." I could hear a disgusted sound in her voice or perhaps even a little sarcasm. The director caught her feeling and quickly tried to explain.

"The people in the embassies in this country are guests of ours, so out of politeness and out of respect, we are asked to only tell them about the Church and what the members are like."

"Yes, I heard all that at the visitor's center."

The director sensed the impatience so hurried on. "We have missionaries in many countries all over the world who tell about the church, but at this time, there are no missionaries in your country."

Immediately, Betty slapped the desk with her hand and asked, "Why not?" The director jumped, surprised at the outburst.

I sensed that Betty was getting past her impatience. She felt as though she was being put off. First it was at the temple—she couldn't go in there; next it was the visitor's center—she learned about the people, but she didn't care about the people. She only wanted to check out that gorgeous structure with the angel on the top.

"The church needs to get permission from their government to send their missionaries there."

"Permission from my government? My husband, at the embassy, is part of the government."

"There is someone in the area of your country you can contact to tell you about the missionaries. Here is his name and telephone number so you can get in touch with him. Tell him of your desires. You can help him get in touch with your government. He will probably listen to your request."

Betty left satisfied.

Now what about Rachel? She was all ready to go to the temple with her nephew, Rhet. Her temple suitcase with her beautiful white gown and clothes was packed, her purse was on her arm, and she was on her way to the door when I called to her, "Your recommend." She continued to the door, so I called again, "Rachel, your recommend!" She knew that it was always in her purse. "Stop!" I called, so she decided that she should check for it again. She reached into her purse; it was not there. She looked in the outside pocket of her purse, in the zippered pocket, in the loose change area—still no luck. I watched her run back to her desk. "Rachel," I called again. "It's in your—" But she cut me right off. Every shelf and drawer was searched, leaving papers scattered everywhere. She knew if she didn't get going, she would be late.

"Rachel, Rachel, listen to me!" I called to her, "Go look in your—" But she cut me right off. She was too frantic to listen to me. Next she ran into the clothes closet and started looking through all the pockets. Not there.

She needed help and she knew it, so she practically skidded to her knees at her bedside and started frantically calling for help. She was talking so fast that I could hardly understand her. "Please help me find my temple recommend, I have looked in my purse, in the side pocket, in the zipper pocket, in the change pocket, in the little desk drawer, in the pencil slot, in my suit pocket, in my . . ."

She was so frantic that she rattled off all the places she had looked. As if we didn't know already.

Out of desperation, I slowly called with all the power I had, while at the same time lightly touching her shoulder. "Be still and listen!" It was like a lightening shock. She actually jumped. She actually heard my voice. She became very still. I gave her mind a picture. As she quietly watched, amazed at what was happening, the temple bag slowly came into view. Through the leather case, she could see her white gown, in the white gown she could see the pocket, and in the pocket was her recommend. Rachel made it in time. It turned out to be a glorious day.

Now as an angel I would like to report that Betty did go forth as had been suggested. By the time the years of her embassy assignment were over and she went home, there were seven hundred members of the Church in her country. Perhaps a temple will be built soon. A temple often follows a gathering.

I am learning more and more every day, putting skills together that work like miracles.

Bibbity-bobbity-boo. —R^2

Beautiful desert
Sifting through the sands of time
Archaeology

Ode to the Pearl of Great Price

From the catacombs of Egypt with its dry, embalming sand,
To the port of New York City within the Promised Land.
I have carried in my bosom a pearl of greatest worth.
To deliver, when the time is right,
To the Saints upon the earth.
The time has been horrendous, I've had centuries to wait.
But my mission was made possible,
'Cause I'm in a "mummy" state.
I lived once as you live now. Loved the wonders of the world
Within Pharaoh's noble palace, where my life was there unfurled.
Some say I am a Christian! I can't blame them for their stand,
For I hold a record written
By the hand of Abraham.

"Who was Abraham?" you asked me. "Why are his words so dear?
Why is his name so honored by the people far and near?"
A chosen man of God was he, a prophet most revered,
A scientist, astronomer,
Who bent Egyptian ears.
Divine promises to Abraham from God, of eternity,
Are passed through gospel blessings and alight on you and me.
Of these blessings and life's doings only Moses gives a view.
But I have the real story
The Lord wants revealed to you.
When my life on this earth ended and my spirit was set free,
The Order of First Burial was performed on what was me.
Thirty days it took to balm me and prepare me for my tomb,
With bitumen and ointments,
And linen from the loom.
With Abraham's papyrus wrapped tight within my chest
I lay in the King's Valley, by the Nile,
To the West.
I am thankful for Lebolo. The Lord made him brave you see,
To rescue the nine mummies, and the Princess, and me.
Shipped down the mighty Nile, then to Ireland by sea,

To the port of New York City,
In 1833.
There M. Chandler paid our passage and took us on a tour.
Then one by one he sold us till there were only four.
That papyrus I squeezed tightly, and at times I held my breath,
For fear the fortune hunters
Would tear it from by chest.
Two years later Prophet Joseph felt a feeling in his breast,
And with the help of brethren,
Paid the money for the rest.
My quest, at last, was over. There stood the prophet dear.
I brought to him the message that the Lord planned him to hear.
Oh what joy filled my bosom! Oh what rapture filled my soul!
"Well done my faithful servant,"
I could hear the echo's roll.
But alas! My joys were ended. Now the Prophet is not alive.
Out of chapters to fill volumes,
He'd translated only five.
From Lucy, then to Emma, On to Mr. Coombs.
From St. Louis to Chicago
(Museums are like tombs).
Perhaps the Saints aren't ready to hear the news I bear.
Perhaps the time is not quite right for Abraham to share
The many truths and wonders the Lord blessed him to see.

Angels Have the Last Laugh

Repent! Repent, my brothers!
Repent, I beg of thee!
I wonder, as I'm lying here, what's to become of
  me.
I hold the record tightly
And pray for me and thee.
Maybe, like Moroni, who wandered to and fro,
And thus preserved his record, then delivered it
  below.
Will I, like he, be sanctioned, to visit on this land
And place my precious record
Into a Prophet's hand?
I know not, but stand faithful and patient to the
  end;
Till I complete the mission He's given me, and
  then
I hope that I will hear His voice in the eternity:
"My good and faithful servant,
Enter unto Me."
From the catacombs of Egypt with its dry, embalm-
  ing sand,
To the port of New York City within the Promised
  Land,
I have carried in my bosom a pearl of greatest
  worth
To deliver, when the time is right,
To the Saints upon the earth.
　—Berta Nielson

Berta testifies that I had a lot to do with this poem. She sat on the side of her bed one evening, and together we wrote it in a very short time. —R^2

In the country store
Dill pickles, leather, coal oil
Alert my senses

The Country Store

I love a country store; my sense of smell comes alive with the smell of dill pickle and peppermint candy, of salted peanuts and Japanese oranges, of coal oil and leather, and of scorched wet clothes too close to the puffing potbellied stove in the corner. That is the kind of store I love. I have dropped in to many a store, but a country store is my favorite. When I drop into a shopping mall, I find that no one knows anyone else. People don't have names, only credit card numbers. But when I drop into the country store in Kimball, everyone knows everyone else. The sound of the crackling fire in winter has dear memories to all who gather in the circle of heat. Each comes for a special reason and then stays to hear what's going on in town. Each contributes their thoughts and plans.

"I just rode three miles to get the mail."

"My children will soon be out of school, and I've come on my horse to ride home with them; that north wind will be pretty cold tonight."

"I had to dig myself out this morning; the snow was halfway up my door."

"This will bring good moisture come spring."

"Yes, I found Lemke, hat still on, leaning over the washtub holding onto the washboard. He had been dead for two days."

"I've started feeding the yearlings. The snow is too deep now for them to find any grass."

"My lake has two feet of ice on it already. When this blizzard lets up, I'm gonna get my ice house filled."

"Did you hear about the three-way deal cut by George and Clint and Ed? George wanted Ed's horse, Ed wanted Clint's horse, and Clint wanted George's horse."

"No, I think that it was Clint that wanted George's horse." Others joined in.

"Wasn't George's horse that sorrel cutter?"

"She was fast at pulling a steer out of the bunch."

"I liked Ed's buckskin."

"It had shoulders like a quarter horse."

"I know that Clint's horse was a big bay horse, tall and sure footed."

"Ed started that trade because he wanted that big horse for his children to ride to school."

"Three of them on the same horse."

"Yeah, he needed a big horse."

The thought of that big horse brought a moment of thoughtful silence, finally broken by . . .

"I thought my Eaton's catalog parcel would be here by now. The missus is anxious to wear her new dress to the shindig Friday night."

"You mean the belly-rubbin' party?" That brought on rounds of laughter as they commented on the husky farmer and his fluffy wife getting close enough to dance. It was a belly rubbin' for sure.

Sounds of laughter continued to fill the little country store as the conversation continued of good times and hard times, of crops, of dances and branding parties, of a new horse and saddle, of weather—last spring and this spring—of lonely times and jolly, and of corn busts and chicken feeds from someone else's garden and coop.

Speaking of chicken feeds—that bachelor, old man Rothe, agreed to have friends drop in with the chickens they had "picked up" for a fried chicken feed. Next morning he noticed that the "picked up" chickens were from his own coop. The guys hanging around the store loved that story.

I love the smell of a garlic dill from the Hutterite colony.[2] It hit me as soon as I dropped in. There was a rock and the round piece of wood on that three-gallon crock to hold the pickles down into the brine. The rock smelled just like the pickles. It even tasted like the pickles. Children would lick that rock if they could get away with it.

The country store shelves were stocked with groceries, Roger's Golden Syrup, hardware, school supplies, jars of candy, harness patching materials, coil oil lamps and wicks, pipe tobacco and cigars, soft drinks in a real icebox, miscellaneous sewing items, candied fruit, and Japanese oranges at Christmastime. It had a gas pump out in front and a government post office in the corner.

I thought that it would be fun to run the post office. There were a lot of little square pigeonholes with name labels. The mail came three times a week. It looked like a fun job to sort the mail and get all the letters in the right place. Some people got lots of mail and some hardly any at all. Could it be that the more letters you write, the more you get back? Or maybe, it could be the bills you have not paid. Yikes!

During school days, the children would pick up the

mail after school and take it home on their school pony. During summer, when there was no school, someone would have to ride the miles into town to pick up the mail. One time, Irene Blinko and a Rothe girl rode to Kimball to get the mail. On the way home, as they were riding lickety-split through the pasture, Emma, the milk cow was standing right in their path.

"Move over, girls," I called out to the racers. But there was so much laughing and riding that they didn't hear me. I even tried to call to the cow—no response there either. I don't know if I have any influence over cows. Never tried it before. I hoped one of them would move. Big Johnny, the horse, was used to whipping down that path because that was his school path every day of the week. I held my breath—which would give? Emma didn't. Johnny didn't. So there was a collision. Both horse and cow went down, and the Rothe girl landed several yards away in a patch of prickly buck brush. The horse got up; the cow got up; the girls got up and crawled back onto the horse, and they raced the rest of the way home, laughing. Nothing fazed them. That was part of everyday country life, and the mail went through one more time.

Randy and Marge were the owners of that post office and the Kimball Country Store. They lived very comfortably in rooms behind the store with their three children. When a customer came into the store a bell would ring, and someone would come out. They were a friendly family, and they were always ready to talk, gossip, or listen. Randy was stocky and always had a grin on his face. Marge was slim and a bundle of dynamite. She was as a good a gabber as you would ever find. It was always fun to stop in at the store.

Periodically, a traveling dentist named Dr. Goering set up shop in that Kimball country store. He set up his drilling machine in Marge's living room, behind the wall of the store. Of course, there was no electricity, so he would pedal the machine with his foot while he would drill on the tooth. His foot would go up and down on the pedal, and the drill would go around and around in the tooth. The pedal was like the ones found on the sewing machines, and the drill—well—made me shiver. It was amazing to me how he could do that—like you rubbing your tummy while you are patting your head. The flying smoke and dental burning smells turned my stomach. The patients called him the "horse" doctor. For sure, he was a rough customer.

Randy also drove the school bus. Now this bus wasn't very fancy—not the yellow bus you picture today. It was simply a green pickup truck with a shell on the back. When the Kimball school closed for lack of students, the remaining students had to be bused five miles to the Aetna school. Now the students put their horses in the country store barn instead of the school yard barn. Randy put benches down the sides of the pickup box for the students to sit on. It would hold ten students.

Randy also raised lots of chickens and pigs—I mean hogs. Weekly he would haul his hogs to market in town in the back of the pickup, then hose out the pig smell, which was supposed to turn the pickup back into a school bus. On the way home, he would pick up the schoolkids. Somehow, the riders got used to that smell and didn't complain—too much.

Christmas was a special time at the Kimball store with Christmas decorations all around. One could buy the ones on the shelf or the ones strung around the store. There were lots of red and green twisted streamers, long silver icicles to hang on the tree, delicate baubles one hardly dared to touch, special string to slip popcorn and cranberries on,

Angels Have the Last Laugh

and angels to top the tree. It was like magic to the two girls who came each day to wait for the school bus. Their names were Betsy and Jill. They tied their horse in the barn behind the store, walked around to the front, and walked into the store. The ring-a-ling notified the owners, who opened their door to see that it was just the girls, early and ready for school.

"Good morning," Marge said and withdrew. She always trusted people coming in and knew the girls would sit by the warm, potbellied stove until it was time for the bus to leave. It was so warm that soon the coats were off, as well as the mitts, scarves, and the wool-lined caps with earflaps. Riding on a horse in the winter was cold.

This routine continued every morning, but it was most interesting at Christmastime as there were so many festive things to look at. Betsy especially loved the candied fruit packages that lined the shelf close by, especially the candied pineapple. She wished that she had some money with her to buy a package of that candied pineapple.

One morning Jill was sick, so Betsy came to school by herself. When Marge heard the ring-a-ling, she said her usual "good morning" and closed the door. As Betsy sat alone by the stove, waiting for the school bus to leave, that candied pineapple caught her eye again. Her taste buds went into full swing. "Oh, but that would taste soooo good," she thought.

I, R^2, came to the rescue. "No, Betsy," I whispered to her. Betsy heard and turned her back to the candied fruit on the shelf.

Soon she was looking at that pineapple again, and I could understand what she was thinking, "Jill is not here."

"No, Betsy," I warned.

"I am all alone in the store," she added.

"No, Betsy, listen to me," I said a little louder.

Betsy's thoughts continued. "No one will ever know."

She was tuning me out. I tried to stand between Betsy and the pineapple on the shelf; it didn't work. She could reach right through me if she wanted. She didn't even know I was there. She overrode her conscience and reached out, picked up a cellophane-wrapped candied pineapple, and quickly stuffed it into her ski jacket pocket.

"Betsy, Betsy, that is not right," I called out. "Quick. Put it back."

This time my message really got to her, but just as she reached into her pocket to undo what she had done, the door opened, and there was Randy, ready to drive to school. It was too late. She had a candied pineapple in her pocket that should not have been there. Her face flushed as she realized what she had done, and now there it was, still in her pocket, and she was on her way to school in the back of the pickup.

She didn't like the thought "pickup," as it reminded her that she had picked up something that did not belong to her, something that she did not pay for. All day long, she thought about it. Her ski jacket was hanging on the peg where her name was, and there was that pineapple in the pocket. I could sense the turmoil she was going through, and I could see that she could hardly concentrate on her studies. She was suffering. Somehow the pineapple didn't tempt her taste buds as it had before in the store.

"I wish that I hadn't picked up that pineapple," she continued reminding herself. "I sure wish that it was not there in my pocket."

I could see that she was really repenting, so I suggested, "You can quietly put it back on the shelf tonight when you get back to the store."

She brightened with the thought. I could see that she

became more relaxed and tended more to her studies.

When she got back to the store, the usual crowd had gathered around the fat-crackling warm stove. There was no way she could sneak that candied pineapple back on to the shelf where it belonged, so it had to go home with her.

Now she had greater worries—would her mother find it? Heaven forbid. She would really be in trouble then. She tried to act natural even though her emotions were frayed. She didn't throw her coat down as she usually did so her mother wouldn't have to remind her to hang it up or would hang it up herself. She made sure that she hung her coat up in the closet nice and straight so that unwanted package wouldn't fall out and be discovered. "I must get rid of it somehow," she said to herself.

"You can put it back on the shelf in the morning," I whispered. She was really tuned in now and looking for a way out.

"Yes," she echoed. "I will put it back on the shelf in the morning. But Jill will be there and may see me. Oh, will this ever end?" she groaned under the load of it.

The thought of that unwanted pineapple in her ski jacket haunted her all night long. She was restless at times. She was sleepless at times. The burden seemed more than she could bear. I allowed her thoughts and dreams to run away with her through the night. Tasty candied pineapple was on her mind the second her head hit the pillow. This was a teaching moment that parents always watch for, but this time the parent did not know, so I moved in.

Luckily, the next morning Jill was still sick, and Betsy rode to school all by herself. She put Johnny, the horse, in the country store barn and walked into the store all by herself. The ring-a-ling brought Marge to the door with her jolly "good morning." Then she was gone. Betsy was alone.

I watched to see what she would do. She looked this

way and that, making sure that no one else was in the store. She quietly, yet quickly, reached into her ski jacket pocket and grabbed that cellophane-wrapped candied pineapple and put it back on the shelf where it belonged. It looked quite worn and wrinkled, but there it was, back on the shelf.

"Good job!" I called to her. I didn't have to call very loud as she was so humble and open for help. She was sorry for that act. That inward guilty feeling and the sting of conscience was gone now. Maybe not completely gone though—every time Betsy saw candied pineapple, the seering remembrance returned, and every time Betsy had the desire to pick up something unpaid for, a crumpled cellophane-wrapped candied pineapple warning appears.

Aah! But I remember how I love a country store. My sense of smell comes alive; the smell of dill pickle and peppermint candy, of salted peanuts and Japanese oranges, of coal oil and leather, and of scorched wet clothes too close to the potbellied stove.

Country stores are classic. —R^2

Mortal body book
Engraved in bones, sinews, flesh
I stand before thee.

My Book of Life

Here I am, my Lord,
The best that I could do.
This body is my book of life which I present to You.
I stand for judgment upon me,
As I've been judged before,
The evidence presented here will open up a door...
... An Eternal door, forever.
Oh! What will be my lot?
So much have I remembered, so much have I forgot.
Know or not, these marks are with me,
Every thought and word and deed;
Some lifted me in ecstasy, some made my poor heart bleed.
My flesh, my bones, my sinews;
Make paragraph, chapter, verse.
My book is open, Thou mayest read to the end, from the first.

Alberta Rothe Nielson

Celestial? Terrestrial? Telestial?
Oh, which one will it be?
Surely not one less that these with buffetings, eternally!
I pray Thee not to read me,
As one who loves and makes a lie,
Or as one honorable but blinded by crafty men on high.
But read me as one righteous,
With hope and charity,
One who loves my fellow man, one who shows much faith in Thee.
My quickened body trembles.
My aura's magnetized.
Is my testimony showing? Can you see it in my eyes?
Oh! What will be the verdict?
Where will my mansion be?
On this, my Day of Judgement—my Book I bare to Thee.
 —Berta Nielson

Berta is good at following my prompting. —R[2]

*Life is what happens
While one is making other plans.
Oh! I love life.*

Befuddled

I had to get a message across—an important message to help someone who was visiting in the Washington, D.C., area. Her name was Dorothy. Dorothy was an avid amateur genealogist researching her family ancestry. There was also another lady visiting in the same area. Her name was Georgia. Georgia was a professional genealogist. She assisted others in this interesting work. Neither knew of the visit of the other, nor did they know each other. Somehow, I had to get them together because Georgia could help Dorothy find her great-grandfather.

In the city of Kensington, Maryland, was a genealogy lab, not too far from Washington, D.C., if you took the metro train. How could I get these two together in Kensington?

First I spoke to Georgia, who was excited about visiting the archives in Washington, D.C., which was part of her reason for being in the capital city. There was so much there to learn about. She wanted to get books and brochures and anything to take home to her own lab. She found that she could use the Internet to access the national archives genealogy library from her computer in Oakland.

"Georgia," I whispered to her mind, "there is another lab in the area."

"I am sure that there are lots of labs in the area," was her answer.

"This is one you should see."

"This is the greatest one in the whole country. This is the one I have looked forward to visiting for a long time." She was quite adamant in her choice.

So I went to the lab director. "That lady should go to Kensington." I could see him wonder why he thought that she should go to Kensington.

"It is small like her library in Oakland," I urged.

He pondered on that thought. "Why not?" he shrugged.

"There is another lab in the area you might find interesting," he suggested to Georgia.

"Why would I want to go there when you have everything here?"

"That library has family pedigrees which we do not have here in the archives. We have lots of names for census, military, citizenship, ship records, Native American and African-American names, but no pedigrees. You will find them in Kensington."

"Where is Kensington?"

"Kensington is in Maryland."

"Isn't that a different state?"

"Yes, but it is easy to get to on the metro."

"What is that?"

"The metro is a commuter train for people in the areas around Washington, D.C. Kensington has a very interesting setup for a small library. Much like the one you have in Oakland."

Instructions were given, and off Georgia went to Kensington on the metro train.

"Whew." I was relieved. Now to get Dorothy there, and not only get her there, but at the same time as Georgia.

Dorothy had an open day and had decided to go sightseeing in Washington, D.C. I had to get her to the Kensington genealogical library. How? I decided to befuddle her mind. I can do that you know, because I am an angel. I can mix up someone's thinking until they cannot make a decision. It is a way to let them know that they are on the wrong track; it is a way to confuse them so much that I can slip into their mind what they are really supposed to do. I started giving her conflicting thoughts. She was picking them up as quick as I could feed them.

She was thinking, "The National Cathedral and the Arlington National Cemetery are what I would like to see. . . . Or should I just take the metro, walk the grassy strip, and see myself in the reflecting pool in the Mall? If I go to the cathedral and the fish market I will have to drive the car. If I go to the Mall, I can take the metro. If I drive I may get lost, but I did want to see the cathedral. Arlington National Cemetery is a must-see. I must go see the changing of the guard, so I will need to take the car. The sentinel guards the Tomb of the Unknown Soldier. Yet the Washington Memorial is an obelisk like the ones in ancient Egypt, but larger. Constitution Hall was owned by the Daughters of the American Revolution. Isn't that ironic? I must see the Washington Memorial!"

Finally Dorothy threw her arms in the air and cried out, "What should I do? I am so confused. Someone please help me decide!"

"Ha, that is me," I gloated. "The genealogy library is close."

"Genealogy library?" she questioned. "Why would I think of genealogy?"

"It is close to here."

"Where?"

"Ask at that corner store up the street from the tall apartment building."

"I'll do that! What a relief!" She paused. "But what about my sightseeing? I want to see the—"

I interrupted her in a hurry with, "How about your great-grandfather?"

"Could I find him here?"

"It's possible." Dorothy grabbed her genealogy bag, which never left her side, even when she traveled, and headed for the car.

Dorothy walked into the genealogical library in Kensington, Maryland. She saw the usual posters and file cabinets, shelves full of books, long tables occupied by many researchers, a couple of film readers and a fiche reader, and smiling specialists ready to help. One guided her to a space beside a lady dressed in red. The lady dressed in red smiled at Dorothy and introduced herself. "Georgia is my name." (You shouldn't be surprised. Of course I led Dorothy to that table. In fact, I led both of them there.)

"I am Dorothy," was the reply.

"I am from Oakland, California," added Georgia. "I am just visiting."

"So am I," Dorothy said then added, "I hear a German accent in your voice. Are you from Germany?"

"Yes, originally, but now I live in Oakland."

"I have ancestors from Germany," Dorothy shared.

"Where?"

"In the lower southeast corner of the original East Germany part, close to Czechoslovakia."

"That's where I'm from. What names are you searching for?"

"Lungwutz, Rothe, Scheunert, and Heuer, to name the main ones."

"Those names are familiar to me."

"I am having trouble finding my Great-Grandfather Rothe. He was born on October 16, 1816."

"Any town name?"

"He landed in New York in September 1849, Country of Allegiance-Saxony. Then I found him in the 1970 census in Wisconsin."

"What was his name?"

"Christian Gottlieb Rothe."

"Where in Saxony?"

"I don't know."

"I remember that Rothe name in Freidersdorf. There are several Freidersdorfs in that area. The Rothe name is quite common in Germany because it means "red" or "redhead" or "ruddy complexioned." Then Georgia said with a very positive and definite tone in her wonderful German accent, "Today we will find him."

Dorothy was ecstatic. "What luck! What a coincidence!"

She called me luck. She called it a coincidence. Little did she realize how hard I had been working to get them together.

Georgia was familiar with genealogy research. She knew how miracles happened. She realized now why she was here—why her thoughts led her to Dorothy.

"Today," Georgia said again with added authority, "we will find him. I will write a letter for you."

"Would you?" Dorothy could hardly believe this was happening. The National Cathedral and Mall were forgotten for the moment.

A letter was written. An answer was received. Christian Gottlieb Rothe was found with a wife and two daughters in Freidersdorf, Bautzen, Saxony, Germany. This brought to light another quest for Dorothy.

Christian Gottlieb Rothe did not bring his wife and daughters to America. Why?

The daughters took their mother's name, Hander. Why?

Were they illegitimate? Were they in line to inherit on their mother's side? Why?

This is what genealogy research is about—always another step to do, always looking for another generation, another sister, another brother. Name by name, step by step, and discovery by discovery the work goes forward. The mortal and immortal string of families is lined up, all connected and joined together in one eternal chain of loved ones.

It is a good feeling to be connected. —R^2

This Leaf

This leaf
From Sacred Grove,
Burst forth from bud at Springtime
To remind us of
Good News;
God still talks to man
And lifts him up
With light of Gospel Plan.
This leaf
From Sacred Grove,
Dancing, shimmering in the breeze.
Posted,
As a sentinel,
Watching from above
Those who enter
In humility and love.
Then, this leaf
From Sacred Grove,
At life's end,
Bears brilliant testimony
And falls
With his watchful brothers;
Blanketing the shrine
In a coat of many colors.
With this leaf

Alberta Rothe Nielson

Sit a while,
And ponder,
In the sacred stillness of
The Grove.
 —Berta

Sitting alone in the Sacred Grove, Berta and I penned this poem. —R²

Sky is the limit
Eagles fly where eagles dare
Mortals dare also

The Crash

The four-seater Cessna 182P plane was losing power. The beautiful autumn-colored treetops were closing in and the upward slope of the canyon was pulling it down. The pilot spent his final moments wrestling with the plane, trying to keep it from nose-diving. All he said to the passengers was, "Brace yourselves; we are going down." The plane hit like a freight train, belly first, on a rocky mountain slope, bounced three times off the sharp rocks, and slid down the tree trunks to a stop. Flash fire filled the cockpit.

I, R^2, was in the plane with them. As a guardian angel, I had been assigned to make a report of any help I could give to people on earth. This is my report of the crash.

It had been such a wonderful weekend: a wedding, a reception, a dance, and a chance to mingle with the families and friends who had gathered from California to Colorado. They met halfway in between in beautiful Utah. The bride's parents and sister lived close by, and the groom's mother drove in from Idaho. The groom's three brothers came from Canada, Idaho, and California. His three sisters came from Colorado and Utah. There was a bridesmaid, also from California, and all the rest of the guests from local towns in the area. Some drove and some flew. All met together in Heber City, a friendly little town in the Uinta National Forest in Utah.

What a group. I was pleased to be one of them. The bride was so beautiful as she approached the white-latticed gazebo, and as the groom waited, I could see his shaking hands clasped behind him. I smiled while I waited, remembering my own wedding long ago.

Yes, my own wedding when I was a young mortal. My memories were coming back strong and clear. I had told my bride, as we were courting, that when the time came for me to say, "I do," I would say, "Ya sure betcha," and she would giggle and smack me on the arm or give me a push. She thought that I was kidding. Maybe I was, but I wanted her to think that I was serious. I tried to give that impression anyway. She must have been somewhat concerned because she brought the subject up quite often. It became quite a game between us. Our wedding day finally came. When I saw her father bringing her to me, I was so nervous. I took her hand to keep mine from shaking. When the time came for her to say, "I do," she said it. I grinned. Then when it came time for me to say, "I do," she gave me that "don't you dare" look out of the corner of her eye. She was remembering that "Ya sure betcha." I grinned. My memory brings back the giggle that escaped her throat when I submissively said, "I do," as I squeezed her hand. It was a very quiet giggle, but it was a giggle, and I wondered if anyone else heard it.

Weddings are important steps in our progression through life. It is the growing up of a man and of a woman and the beginning of a new family. This process evolves

Angels Have the Last Laugh

until generations are all joined together in one sacred chain. The wedding today had now joined two separate families—the bride's and the groom's. It is a wonderful plan. My job is to help families like this, to be around when needed, and to give counsel and comfort.

By morning, all the festivities were over, and the bride and groom were happily on their way to Hawaii. Imagine, a honeymoon in Hawaii. I should have gone with them, but somehow I felt a need to stick around here. The local family members and guests were saying their good-byes and returning to their homes. The groom's family was gathered at the small local airport to say goodbye to the groom's sister Verla and her husband, Bart, and their two young boys—eleven and seven. Bart was a professional pilot. He had rented a plane in Colorado and flew his family to the Heber City airport for the wedding. Now they were fueled up and ready to go back home.

Such a beautiful fall morning in the mountains caught the eyes of all. Daniels Canyon especially was dressed in many bright colors of mahogany, oak, aspen, and tall, browning grasses. The bright sun and blue sky were towering over this seemingly sugar-coated landscape. "Surely," I thought, "Hawaii couldn't be better than this."

Verla's brother Rex spoke up. "Bart, before you go, how about taking us on a sightseeing flight up those canyons?" Many voices chimed in. Who to take? The decision fell on three: Rex, who had suggested it; Gary, who had been the best man at the wedding; and Sissy, for a birthday present because she had turned sixteen just two days before. All climbed in the little Cessna, and they were off. I crawled in with them. I have no weight in the mortal sense of mass, so a fifth passenger was no problem. We circled the valley along the beautiful mountainsides and finally disappeared from the view of the family at the

81

airport—disappeared in the hazy hot sun and blue sky.

As we proceeded up Daniels Canyon I noticed that Bart was working a lot of switches. Gary commented, "The trees seem to be getting pretty close."

No answer from the pilot. He was busy.

There was some noticeable coughing of the motor. Rex thought, "Are we running out of gas?" That could not be because he remembered that thirty-one gallons of 100 percent octane fuel had been loaded at the airport. The tank was full. "What is causing the sputtering?" he asked.

No comment from the pilot. He was very busy. He kept working the switches. I sensed trouble. I checked the workings of the plane. I could see through the metal into the exhaust system. Something was flipping back and forth, even shutting down at times. I held my breath. What could I do? I was here to help people, but I was helpless here. I had no magic to move that mechanical flapping. I could do nothing about this problem. Oh, if only I could move that blockage. That sort of thing was not in my power.

Bart was leaning forward and going through all the emergency procedures possible to keep the nose up. He was very busy, which seemed to keep him calm. "Where to land?" he thought. Up ahead he could see a bare spot with no trees. It was steep, though. It looked like a winter avalanche had moved down the face of the mountain, wiping out the trees. It was rocky, but better than the trees.

Finally he professionally announced, "Brace yourselves; we are going down." I tried to get Bart to straighten up and brace himself too, but he was too busy being a responsible pilot and could not hear me. He fought that plane right to the end—keeping that nose up. His skills brought that little Cessna in on its belly.

On contact, the pilot lost his life. He didn't brace himself like I told him to. Luckily the passenger door had popped open, and Rex fell out head first. Gary, sitting behind the pilot, tried to get out, but he couldn't. He couldn't figure out what was holding him down. It was hot in there, and he was burning. He looked at Sissy, who sat in the backseat by him, and saw her undo her seat belt. "Aah! That's it—my seat belt." He pushed her out and then undid his own seat belt and scrambled out. Rex, who was riding in the front, was hanging out of the door headfirst because his foot was caught in the seat belt. He couldn't get it out, and he couldn't lift himself uphill to release the seat belt. Gary saw the trouble and reached through the wall of flames to help him. He couldn't get it undone. He moved out because his face and arms were on fire and then moved in again. Rex knew his feet were burning, so he finally gave a jerk and out came his foot. It actually slithered out with no skin. Gary pulled him away from the fiery inferno. Rex ran around the plane for Bart. It was too late. The cockpit was full of flames, and Bart was not moving. Rex bowed his head, and the tears flowed.

By now, the mahogany and aspens were on fire, and the dry, browning grasses were leading the flames up the mountainside at a running rate. There was no shade for cover. I saw a small group of aspen over in the middle of the rough rocks, away from all the fires, so I brought it to Gary's attention. He moved Rex and Sissy there. It was not much shade—just a little—but they were away from the burning forest. They were hurting so badly. Their burns were unbearable. The hot sun reflecting off the hot rocks and the heat from the plane and forest fires added to their pain. Yet they were lucky to have found that little spot of refuge.

Rex was the worst with his face and arms and legs burned. Gary's face and arms were burned. Sissy had one burned arm and a black eye. Gary was afraid that Rex was a goner, so he took off his shirt and jeans to cover him from the hot sun.

"Someone will come soon," Gary told them. "The rangers will see the smoke and be up here soon." They did not come.

I rushed down to the ranger station and told them about the fire. They looked up and saw the smoke, so they sent a plane up that way. They did not spot the downed plane nor the people waiting there because the plane was covered by walls of fire and the injured were hidden under the small tuft of aspens. I tried frantically to show them to the wreckage, but they decided the fire had been started by campers or hikers. They turned back to get a fire-fighting crew on the move. They would not listen to me.

I went back to the waiting people. They huddled in that little clump of trees and talked, and cried and yelled and cussed. "Where is our help?"

"Gary," I said, "we need to get some help for Rex."

"I know that for sure," he told me.

"Do you remember flying over a road down at the bottom of the canyon?"

"Yes, I saw it from the plane. We even followed it for a while."

"You can make it if you try. I think that it is only a couple of miles."

"Rex is in such terrible condition that I am afraid to leave him. I must keep him awake and talking, or he will be gone."

"Sissy can talk to him," I said.

Gary turned to Sissy. "Sissy, I am going for help. Will you talk to Rex and keep him awake?"

Sissy was hot and red faced. Her arm felt like it was still burning. She had no more tears. She had no more screams nor cries for help. Her quota was all used up. "Yes, I can do that," she whispered.

Gary took off at a run, stumbling over the hot, sharp rocks, through the aspens and tall grass, and down through the canyon trail. He ran and ran. His brother was depending on him. I kept guiding him to the best trails. "Run on this side of the canyon. Now on the other side," I told him. I could tell that he was not thinking about himself at all, nor about the scratchy bushes on his blackened face and arms. He only thought of his brother and niece, sitting there in the hot rocks by the burning plane and forest.

I saw a lady hiking with her dog on one of the mountain trails. I rushed to her. "Hurry to the car." I called. She turned and wondered where the thought came from. "Get your dog in the car, hurry."

Then she heard a real call. "Help! Help! Help!" She looked up and saw a hiker—at least she thought that it was another hiker. Then she noticed that he was about naked. He was running at full speed. Now he was close enough so she could see that his face and arms were charred.

"Oh," she gasped, "what is happening?"

"Where is the road?" the runner called, never slowing his pace.

"Just on the other side of those willows," she pointed. "I will take you there as soon as I get my dog in the car." When she turned back, he was gone. He ran straight through the willows—the branches lashing at his wounds. By the time she got to the road, Gary was standing out in the middle stopping cars.

He was majestic. He was standing there, black and charred, wearing only his boxers and cowboy boots. He was waving down the cars and asking for help. One car stopped and wanted to take him to the hospital, but he would not go until he found help for Rex and Sissy. A Jeep stopped. Two men were coming home from fishing. They said they would go get someone to go up there. Gary insisted that they go up there right now. "You two can carry Rex, and Sissy can walk." He told them. "Go now. Please go now." He was pleading. "You can drive the Jeep up about one mile and then hike the rest. There is a trail. Go!"

Another car stopped. It was a nurse who had once worked in a burn center. Immediately she jumped out of the car because she recognized Gary's plight. "I am a burn nurse; come with me." She insisted, but he refused until the fishermen promised they would go up the canyon. They went. The moment Gary got into the nurse's car, he passed out.

By this time, the word was out, and Verla and her boys, along with other members of the family, were at the Wasatch County Hospital in Heber City. They got there just in time to see Gary on a stretcher on his way to the university burn center. When Gary saw his mother he said, "I'm okay, Mom. Don't worry." She reached out and touched his bandaged body. Then he was gone.

As the whole family gathered, the rangers reported, "The rescuers found three people at the crash site. Two are alive, and one is not." The family wondered who it was. Was it Bart, the pilot; Rex, the brother; or sweet Sissy?

They waited. I waited too, trying to comfort where I could. Sissy's mother was crying and was beside herself. I went to her and said, "Go to your little children. They need you." That sobered her. She saw them huddled together wondering, what was going on. She ran to them and held them tight.

Verla was holding her sons' hands and walking from one ranger to another, asking and waiting for more news. It came. "Two people are being helicoptered to the burn center in Salt Lake City. The pilot is not one of them." Verla held her sons tight. I put my arms around them. They were so stunned that they could not feel me, yet I could feel them draw strength from me. I could sense that Verla was expecting this news because she was tearless. She had already steeled herself against it. She took her sons to her mother's car to drive to the university burn center.

"May I drive?" she asked.

Her mother looked surprised. "Are you . . . ?"

"I need to keep my mind busy." It was a statement. She drove. The young boys sat quietly in the back. What can one say? It was a time of stunned silence. As they moved down the highway, Verla revealed to her mother what she was thinking. "I guess I am a widow." It was a shocking statement, but delivered as a matter of fact.

"Oh," I thought, "there will be some tough times ahead for this brave young woman."

The burn center was a hive of activity. Three members of one family in beds, each in a different room, to keep infection away. A new gown was required every time anyone entered one of the rooms. Sissy—black left eye, left arm burned, 6 percent burned. Gary—face and both arms burned, 13 percent burned. Rex—face, both arms and both legs burned, 25 percent burned. He was out completely. He had a neck brace and was put under chemical paralysis for fear of fracture. The rule of thumb for the length hospital stay for burns is that the percent of burn equals the number of days in the hospital. The heavily bandaged burned arms and legs were spread-eagled out. Both brothers had tubes in their mouths, which made talking impossible.

When Gary awoke he could not talk because of the tubes in his nose and mouth. He told his family his story through his written messages.

Now I must leave you with some closure.

The court declared mechanical failure on the rental plane in favor of the family.

Bart was a true pilot who gave his life to save his passengers. He fought that plane and kept its nose up all the way down. The family will be grateful forever.

Many days of the terrible treatment were spent on skin grafting. It is the most excruciating pain that one can imagine. There must be a better treatment. Although I am an engineer, I can be influential in developing a new method. It is called innovative engineering.[3] Specialists in different professional fields put ideas together. Sometimes the ideas are even serendipity surprises. That is what modern technology is about. May God be with me in this project.

After continued surgeries of skin grafting on both arms, Gary developed a series of blood clots. Two years later, one finally reached his heart. He died at age thirty-eight.

Rex had severe skin grafting surgeries on both legs and arms, even on his fingers and around his fingernails. He now has no wrinkles on his knuckles. The prospect of losing a leg turned into the prospect of losing a foot, and finally became the loss of a toe joint. The foot is permanently injured, but he can still stand tall. He now lives with Post Traumatic Stress Disorder.

Sissy is as good as new. She wears the scars of skin grafting on her arm with dignity. Luckily the scars from the new skin they used hides under her swimsuit.

We lost Bart—a hero. Utah forest rangers were sur-

prised that he could save all of his passengers in such a rugged canyon. I love this little family. Should they ever call on me for help, I will be there to whisper and guide.
—R²

Endnotes
1. Canadian couch.
2. A Hutterite is a member of an Anabaptist community now living in communistic rural settlements in Alberta, Saskatchewan, and the northwestern United States.
3. A presentation by the author made at an engineering conference in Puerto Rico.

Epilogue

"Randolf Rippenhoffer, R^2, *come home.*" I heard my name being called.

"Come home?" I asked.

"Yes, R^2. Come home."

"Why? Is something wrong?"

"No, not wrong."

"I did help Henry this time, didn't I?"

"Yes, you did help Henry this time. You helped him last time too, as best you could, but he had to do his part too. This time he was ready to listen to you."

Then in a questioning tone, the voice added, "Are you ready for a little R & R?"

"Yes, I would like that. Yet please know that I am really enjoying this assignment. It is so surprising how I can laugh and visit with those whom I meet, and how satisfying it is to really make a difference for good in their lives."

"Which experience was your favorite?"

"The little green house comes to mind first, yet I did love the last chicken—it really made me chuckle. That butcher really put himself in an awkward position."

"I am glad that you were there at the right moment. It was an experience that I hope he remembers for future sales."

"Also, I was pleased how I could befuddle the minds of Dorothy and Georgia to get them together, and how I guided Grace to get her mother's temple work done."

"I saw that," the voice said with a laugh, "and I noticed that Grace got pretty disgusted with you when she thought that she should chop kindling for the rest of her life." They laughed.

"I was so relieved when she finally dared to pray."

"Did you learn any new skills this time?"

"Oh, yes. One was the ability to really shock Rachel to get her attention."

"And then you gave her a video—that was a new skill."

"It was awesome."

"Now, R^2, How about a change?"

That caught my attention, and I paused to listen.

"There are animals."

"Animals! You said animals." The cow on the trail came to mind. Maybe I could have influenced her after all and saved the girls from that crash.

He read my mind. "Yes, the girls and the horses were too involved to hear you."

"They were racing at breakneck speed."

"Well, R^2, take a break; then will you be ready to go again?"

"Yes, yes. Thank you very much. I am ready to travel home."

About the Author

Alberta Nielson is an engineer, speaker, and author. Her first book was *Angels Can Laugh Too*.

Alberta was born in Alberta, Canada, and now lives in Salt Lake City. She has seven children and twenty grandchildren. At age fifty, she started college at Brigham Young University, earning her bachelor's and master's degrees in engineering. She worked for Rockwell International and Lockheed Martin. Her last project was designing experiments for a nuclear reactor.

She has given workshops in California, New York, Puerto Rico, and several cities in Idaho and Utah. One of her most popular workshops, "Breaking the Veil of Dreams—If You Can Dream It, Do It," encourages women to push out of their comfort zone and into the many new experiences life can bring.

Now that Berta is retired, she spends her time writing family histories, true-life stories, tall tales, and spiritual happenings.